Lottie Biggs is NOT Tragic

or
Random Reflections
and
Philosophical Thoughts
of
Charlotte B. Biggs

'I am just going to write
because I cannot help it'

Charlotte Brontë

Hayley Long was born in Ipswich ages ago. She studied English at university in Wales, where she had a very nice time and didn't do much work. After that she spent several years in various places abroad and had a very nice time and didn't do much work then either. Now Hayley is an English teacher and works very hard indeed. She lives in Norwich with a rabbit called Irma and a husband.

Lottie Biggs is Not Tragic

Hayley Long

MACMILLAN CHILDREN'S BOOKS

First published 2011 by Macmillan Children's Books

This edition published 2014 by Macmillan Children's Books
a division of Macmillan Publishers Limited
20 New Wharf Road, London N1 9RR
Basingstoke and Oxford
Associated companies throughout the world
www.panmacmillan.com

ISBN 978-1-4472-6555-9

1 3 5 7 9 8 6 4 2

A CIP catalogue record for this book is available from
the British Library.

Printed and bound by CPI Group (UK) Ltd, Croydon CR0 4YY

Part 1

I am what I am

Just when I thought I knew everything about me that there is to know, I have gone and shocked myself. I am potentially the next Lady Gaga. I've written my very own chart-topping smash hit pop classic, which succeeds in being both poppy and light and deep and meaningful all at the same time. When you consider that I gave up music at the end of Year 9, this is actually quite incredible. My song goes like this:

I am what I am
And what I am is blatantly magic
I dye my own hair
Sometimes it's lush
Sometimes it's tragic
And it's my Wales that I want to have a cracking time in
It's my Wales
So it's not a place I'm going to hide in
Life's not worth two twigs
Unless I can shout out
I AMMMM LOTTIE BIGGS.

Even though I've borrowed the basic idea, rhythm and structure from a song that already exists, over half of the words are entirely my own. And despite the fact that they are probably the best words I've ever written, I intend to keep them completely to myself. I wrote this song for my own personal satisfaction and so that I can sing it secretly whenever I'm in need of an emergency ego boost. Recently, this has been a fairly frequent occurrence because I'm just approaching the end of my first term in Year 11 and, as anybody with half a head knows, Year 11 is an extremely stressful experience.

I'M not even going to show it to my best friend, Goose McKenzie. Or to Gareth Stingecombe, my future husband and life partner. It's not that I'm a particularly secretive and private person but some things – like my Facebook password, my Justin Timberlake lucky knickers, my Prince Harry scrapbook and all of my personal bodily regions –

are strictly for my eyes only. My musical masterpiece is among them.

But I might show it to Elvis Presley. I think he'd appreciate it. I'm not talking about the real Elvis Presley, of course. I'm talking about a fat looky-likey who spends half his time asleep on a public bench in the middle of Whitchurch village, which is the part of Cardiff that I live in. *Our* Elvis is scruffy and scatty and drinks more cans of beer than he totally ever should. Even so, I still like him. This is partly because of his voice. It's big and booming and completely hits all the right notes in all the right places so that when he sings he sounds exactly like the original American Elvis – just with a strong Welsh accent. Mostly though, I like him because he has introduced me to the fascinating subject of philosophy. Sometimes it's fair to say that intellectual enlightenment can come from the very place that you'd least expect it.

It all started this evening on my way home from school. I was feeling quite buzzy and brilliant. There is no mystery surrounding my good mood. I can explain it in two very sexy words.

Gareth Stingecombe.

I'd just spent eighty quality minutes watching him run around in a rain-drenched rugby shirt.

Even though it's just turned December and pitch-black by half past three, I'd stayed behind to watch him play rugby for the school team. I wasn't the only Dag[1] hanging about. There were quite a few of us. We'd picked a good game to watch because Gareth was AMAZING. He was charging all over the rugby pitch with the ball clutched tightly to his manly chest, and the rain was soaking into his shirt and making it cling to his body in a very striking and memorable manner. I enjoyed the game a lot. But the best bit came just before the final whistle. Gareth made a spectacular swerving run the entire length of the pitch and then threw his whole body over the touchline to score the most magnificent try I have personally ever witnessed. I was so proud that I thought my heart was going to pop. Before I could get a grip of myself, I started jumping up and down and waving my umbrella about and shrieking:

'GO GAZZY

GO GAZZY

OH OH OH OH

GO GAZZY

---

[1] Our school rugby team isn't supported by Wags because none of the players are legally old enough to be married. It's supported by Dags. Dads and Girlfriends.

GO GAZZY

IT'S GETTING HOT IN HERE SO TAKE OFF ALL YOUR CLOTHES.'

It wasn't quite as good as my chart-topping smash hit pop classic but it did nicely sum up my feelings at that particular time.

One of the dads standing close by me shook his head and said, 'Not appropriate, love,' and then he called out to Gareth, 'Nice work, sunshine.' Gareth nodded and said, 'Ta,' and then he looked over at me, raised his hand to his mouth and blew me a kiss. Right there. In front of all those miserably appropriate and unsexy dads. Even though I am only five foot and half an inch, I suddenly felt about twelve feet tall.

When the game ended, Gareth jogged over to me and kissed me carefully on the cheek. 'I won't touch you,' he said. 'I'm a bit muddy.' As if to prove the point, he put his head on one side, gave it a shake, and a clod of earth fell out of his ear. 'Thanks for coming. I always play better when you come and watch.'

'Wow,' I said and grinned, tactfully ignoring the ear mud. 'That's so random because I'm utterly pointless when *I* play sport.'

Gareth wiped more mud off his eyebrow. 'Do you want

me to walk you home? I've gotta have a post-match team talk with Coach Jenkins and the boys and then I'll probably need a quick shower but it'll only take a minute.'

'Nah,' I said. 'Best be off. My mum might be wondering where I am.'

'See you tomorrow then,' said Gareth and carefully gave me another non-muddy kiss. As our faces parted, his eyes lingered on mine and, just for a moment, I was helplessly captivated in a highly romantic eye-lock. Gareth has very beautiful green eyes and when I look deeply into them, it's very difficult for me to keep a clear thought in my head. For that second, it was as if all the dads and girlfriends and rugby boys and drizzle had magically evaporated. Without really knowing why, I held my breath – and when Gareth opened his mouth to speak, I just knew he'd say something that would perfectly capture the moment. In a weirdly wobbly voice, he said, 'I love Usain Bolt.' And then he coughed and started frowning down at his rugby boots.

'*Who?*' I said.

'Usain Bolt,' said Gareth, coughing again and clearing his throat. 'The athlete. I love the speed and commitment that he displays on the running track.'

'Oh,' I said, slightly confused. The romantic spell was well and truly broken.

'No worries,' said Gareth, and then he turned and jogged off towards the changing rooms.

Gareth is extremely gorgeous. He is also slightly odd sometimes.

And it was not long after this gorgeous and slightly odd moment that I spotted Elvis. He was dancing down the road towards me and singing 'I Am What I Am' into the pointy end of his traffic cone. I had one of my earphones in but I could still hear him because his voice gets incredibly loud when it's combined with this particular piece of highway safety equipment.[2]

But it wasn't the traffic cone trick which caught my attention because I've seen Elvis do this a million times before. It was his T-shirt. It had something written on it. I slowed down to a stop in front of him and frowned.

'*I drink therefore Ian,*' I said, flipping out the other earphone of my MP3 player. And then I frowned again. 'That doesn't make any sense.'

Elvis stopped singing and said, 'Holy Moley! Don't they bother to teach you lot to read any more?' He tucked his traffic cone under his arm and smoothed out his T-shirt so that I could read it better. He looked like this.

---

[2] I once asked my double-science teacher, Mr Thomas, why this happens and he gave me a very thorough reply. It went something like this:

'Well, Lottie, there are two possible explanations. One is that your friend Elvis is effectively using the cone as an amplifier by touching it with his lips and causing it to vibrate. This then increases the efficiency with which the sound waves are transferred into the air and, thus, makes them louder. However, a second and more likely explanation is that it is simply a result of concentration. Instead of the sound energy being spread out in *all* directions, it is concentrated through the cone in just that *single* direction, making it seem very much louder – but only for those at the opposite end of the cone. Does that answer your question?'

I said, 'Yes.' Because it did.

I frowned *again* and said, '*I drink therefore I am*. It still doesn't make much sense.'

Elvis Presley put the traffic cone on the pavement and said, 'Crikey O'Reilly! You kids know nothing! This T-shirt is *obviously* a reference to the great seventeenth-century philosopher René Descartes. Surely you've heard of him?'

I shook my head.

Elvis looked unimpressed, shook his own head and muttered, 'Jeez Louise!' Then he said, 'Descartes once famously said *I think therefore I am* – meaning that even though we can ask questions about absolutely everything, the one thing that we *can't* question is our own existence –

otherwise how the heck would we be asking all these questions in the first place?'

For a moment, I stared at Elvis in gobsmacked silence. This was a lot to take in. Especially after watching Gareth run around in a rain-drenched rugby shirt. When I'd recovered enough to speak, I said, 'Since when have you been into all this deep stuff?'

Elvis rolled his eyes and said, 'I had a life before I turned into Elvis, didn't I? I studied philosophy in my younger days.'

'Huh?' I said. This was all just getting weirder and weirder.

Elvis looked shocked. '*Philosophy*. You know, the pursuit of wisdom and knowledge?'

I scratched my head. I had *heard* this word before. I think I may even have *used* it once or twice. But that doesn't mean I knew what it *meant*. Still confused, I said, 'We don't pursue wisdom and knowledge in my school.'

Elvis tutted. 'Evidently,' he said. And then he zipped up his jacket, picked up his cone and walked off.

I watched him go. My head was spinning out like a spin dryer on a spin cycle. I wasn't used to this. Usually, Elvis just sings songs or else dances by himself on the traffic island. I've never heard him talk about the pursuit of wisdom and knowledge before! I was so spun out and surprised that, all the way home, our conversation kept playing over and over in my head like a track on my MP3 player that had got stuck on repeat.

When I got back, my mum wasn't in. I looked at my phone and there were four messages telling me that she'd be working late and that I should help myself to the remains of the shepherd's pie she'd made yesterday. I wrinkled up my nose and wondered if this had anything to do with Detective Sergeant Giles. He and my mum work together. They're both police officers in the same building and I think he takes up far too much of her time. He's always making her work extra hours and phoning her up at home and, as a result, my poor mum doesn't have any kind of social life. To be honest, I don't like Detective Sergeant Giles. In the summer, there was a very embarrassing situation involving me, him and various pairs of stupid stolen shoes. I can't say any more on this subject because I don't like to talk about it.

Still wrinkling my nose, I took just enough money for a home-delivery pizza from the emergency fund that we keep hidden in an old toffee tin in the back of the kitchen cupboard. As I said before, my mum is a police officer. She does a very difficult and demanding job and has made a massive contribution towards making Cardiff a safer and more pleasant place to live. But this doesn't change the fact that her shepherd's pie tastes of phlegm.

After ordering my pizza, I went upstairs and switched on my computer and typed the name *Rennay Daycarte* into Google. A message came up telling me that it didn't match one single document. I tried again with *Renay Daycart*. This time, the first item that came up had the heading *I think therefore I am*. It also gave me the proper spelling of René's name – which was very helpful because, unlike Lottie Biggs, it's not the sort of name that is written at all how you think it should be.

I sat and read about René Descartes for nearly an hour. I learned a lot about him. For a start, he looked quite similar to this.

Admittedly, it's not a look that would work well nowadays but, once upon a time, it was probably perfectly OK to rock this style in places like France.

Secondly, I discovered that René is widely regarded to be the first modern thinker. When you bear in mind that he wasn't born until the year 1596, this is actually fairly freaky. I've no idea what was going on in the heads of all the people who were around before this date but, whatever it was, it wasn't modern thinking.

And finally, I discovered that I actually quite like this

dead French philosopher. Even though there's a lot of very boring and complicated stuff written about him on the internet, the truth is that René Descartes achieved eternal fame and respect for stating the most simple and obvious fact that can ever be stated:

I THINK THEREFORE I AM

Quite simply, thinking was his way of knowing that he definitely existed. I suppose it was also his way of trying to make sense of everything else.

And then, because I needed to make sure that *I* definitely existed, I opened a new document on my computer and wrote my *I am what I am* song. And when I'd finished writing that, I opened *another* new document and started writing about Gareth's wet rugby shirt and my journey home from school and Detective Sergeant Giles and various other random reflections and philosophical thoughts.

Now normally when I write, it's because I've been told I've got to do it. By my English teacher. Or by Blake, my mental health counsellor, who has been helping me sort out all the weird stuff that sometimes gets cluttered up in my head.

But this time, I don't need any excuses.

The words written here exist only because I have chosen to write them.

I suppose I might even go as far as to conclude this:

But that's enough deep stuff for the moment. I've just heard the doorbell and, quite frankly, it's a tragic person who fills their head with mind-bending philosophical ideas when they could be filling their stomach with an eight-inch chilli beef pizza instead.

traumatIC faCe INCIDeNTs

My friend Goose McKenzie is an extremely cool individual. Like Elvis Presley, she is also capable of random moments of startling wisdom. Goose once told me that everybody in the entire world can be neatly slotted into one of the following three style categories:

> Type A people are masters of fashion.
> Type B people are slaves to fashion.
> Type C people are actually from another planet and have no idea what the word 'fashion' actually means. René Descartes was probably one of these.

Goose said that she is definitely a Type A person. At the time she told me this, I could only agree with her. We were sitting inside Pat's Plaice sharing a plate of chips, and Goose was wearing some crazy new leg-wear and a hand-knitted Peruvian poncho. She'd also given herself a massive comb-over and blow-dried her hair until it was so huge that she looked like a Woolly Mammoth in wet-look leggings. In comparison, everyone else in the chip shop looked rather bland.

When I asked her which type of person she thought *I* was, Goose had paused for a fraction too long before deciding that I'm probably on the cusp of Types B and C. After she'd told me this, I'd called her a crusty hedge-pig and sprinkled vinegar in her hair and then Goose had stood up, yanked wide the neck of my school jumper and shaken half a tonne of salt down my back – and then Pat had shouted at us from behind his fish counter and told us both to get out. If I'm really honest though, it's hard to totally disagree with her. Whichever way you look at it, Goose *is* a very fashionable individual. And a free thinker. And a Kool-with-a-K-Coolio-who-is-cooltastically-cool-for-cats-and-way-too-cool-for-school. She is even an Existentialist Absurdist. Which basically means that her outlook on life can be summed up like this:

Life is essentially meaningless. Especially when you're in a maths lesson!

In my experience, not many fifteen-year-olds even know what an Existentialist Absurdist is, but Goose does because she blatantly is one. That's how clever and cool and *A-Type* fashionable my friend Goose actually is.

But I have to say that even Goose has shown that she is unable to appreciate the finer aspects of philosophy. This morning, as I walked to school with her, I told her about my conversation with Elvis Presley and how he'd introduced me to the fascinating theories of René Descartes. I was feeling quite bright and energized because it was a Friday and I was feeling that funky Friday fever. Also, I'd just eaten a piece of chocolate in the shape of a shooting star I'd found behind door two of my Advent calendar. It's possible that I was a bit over-emotional about Descartes. I talked about him almost all the way to school and then, finally, as we neared the school gates, I summed up my thoughts by saying, 'I mean . . . can you imagine it, Goose? One day, René just decided that the only thing he had to believe was that he existed – and everything else was potentially a load of hogwash. Can you imagine writing something like that over all your exam papers? That would be well funny!'

I don't think Goose was as interested as I was. She said, 'René who?' and then she said, 'I'm not being funny, Lotts, but are you aware that you're having a Traumatic Face Incident?'

'Huh?' I said.

'An unidentified facial object has landed on you – just *here*,' she said, tapping the end of her own nose as if she were my mirror. 'It looks helluva angry. Honestly, it's like a panic button. Do you want to borrow my concealer stick?'

I said, 'What? No way!' And then I touched my nose and experienced that upsetting bruise-like sensation that could only mean one thing – a freshly emerged evil red zombie had taken root on my face.

So I wailed, 'Oh my God, how the heck did that get there? It wasn't there when I washed my face this morning.'

Spots are like that. Like toothache and timed essays, they spring up on you from out of nowhere and you just have to keep calm and deal with them. Taking a few quick deep breaths to dispel any possible panic attack, I patted all my pockets until I found my *own* concealer stick and then I dealt with it. And if that sounds like I've got some weird issue about using Goose's make-up, I should just point out that I was, in fact, thoughtfully avoiding any awkwardness which might arise in the event of my facial deformity exploding on concealer contact.

When we reached the main building, Goose said, 'See you soon, big baboon,' and I said, 'I doubt it, dimwit,' and then we hugged and parted to go our separate ways. I'm in hardly any classes with Goose. Only English and science. I'm not even in the same registration group. Personally, I think my school has a deliberate and sneaky policy of keeping close personal friends isolated at opposite ends of the building. I have no idea why. It's a commonly accepted truth that all teenagers produce superior work when they're in a relaxed and friendly environment and can sit next to whoever they like and chat. It also helps if we can chew gum. Anyone with half a head knows this.

Giving Goose a final wave, I made my way to the tuck shop where I guessed I'd find my future husband and life partner, Gareth Stingecombe, somewhere near the front of the queue. Sure enough, he was being served just as I arrived. When he saw me, he said, 'Biggsy babes!' and winked in a way that made my knees go wonky. After paying his money to Mr Doughnut,[3] he hurried towards me with two steaming paper bags in his hands.

'Biggsy babes,' he said again and pushed one of the paper bags into my hands. 'I've bought you a December Special. You can tell Chrimbo's just around the corner cos Doughnut's started selling turkey baguettes.'

I peered into the bag and inspected the sandwich inside. The bread was already turning soggy from the hot filling and gloopy cranberry sauce. Turkey-smelling steam rose up through the cold air and hit my nostrils. It made me feel a bit sick to be honest. Politely, I took a small nibble and then I carefully re-wrapped the sandwich and put it into the pocket of my coat. Usually, I don't bother wearing a coat because coats have a tendency to make me look utterly unhip like a straighty one-eighty. Which is not symmetrically

---

[3] Mr Doughnut isn't Mr Doughnut's proper name. He's actually called Mr Dougherty and he runs our tuck shop in his spare time. And as he makes quite a lot of doughnuts and sells quite a lot of doughnuts and eats quite a lot of doughnuts, it's hardly surprising that we've tweaked his surname a fraction. Incidentally, Mr Doughnut is stick thin and doesn't actually resemble a doughnut in the slightest.

square but definitely slightly squircle, if you know what I mean. Even so, there are some occasions when refusing to wear a coat just for the sake of fashion would be utterly stupid. A freezing December day in Cardiff is precisely one of them. Also, I need a coat which has reasonably deep pockets because I've recently stopped using a school bag. In my opinion, school bags make you look like you're a Type B person who is desperately trying to be a Type A.

'Don't you want it?' asked Gareth anxiously.

'Of course I do, Gazzy,' I said, 'But I'll eat it later when it's not burning my fingerprints off.'

Gareth is a very hunky and chunky individual who requires a lot of fuel to get him through the day. Even though we've officially been an item for practically five months, he often forgets that I only eat about one-twelfth of the amount of food that he does and that I can't cope with turkey and cranberry sauce baguettes at five past eight in the morning. I didn't want to hurt his feelings by appearing ungrateful though because it was, after all, sweet of him to be thinking about my dietary requirements.

'Ta, Gaz,' I said and turned to give him a turkey-flavoured kiss. But then, before I even had a chance to shut up my big mouth, I stopped and said, 'Oh my God! Did you know that you're having a totally intense Traumatic Face Incident?'

He was as well. The most humongous zombie I've ever seen was growing on his chin. I don't know how I hadn't noticed it before. For half a second, I thought it was quite sweet that we'd both been blighted by spots at the same time but then I thought about it a bit more and decided that it was actually quite disgusting.

Gareth said, 'Huh?'

'You've got a whopping great zit, Gaz,' I said. And, helpfully, I tapped my own chin as if I were his mirror and said, 'Right *here*.'

'No, I haven't,' said Gareth, his face turning the same colour as his cranberry sauce – and then he touched his chin and frowned.

'I told you so!' I said triumphantly.

Gareth's frown deepened and in a slightly snappy voice, he said, 'All right, Biggs, there's no need to sound so flipping chuffed!' And then he shook his head at me and bit sulkily on his sandwich.

I felt bad then. I can be a heartless wench sometimes, I honestly can. Sometimes, stuff just comes out of my mouth without having passed through a Stupid Filter first. In an effort to put things right, I said, 'Do you want to borrow my concealer stick?' And then, to be extra nice, I added, 'I'll do it for you if you like. I could get that bad boy sorted out for you in a matter of seconds.'

Instead of answering me, Gareth spluttered on his turkey baguette. I thumped him on the back and said, 'Do you want me to go and get Mr Doughnut?' This isn't as random as it sounds. As well as being in charge of the tuck shop, Mr Doughnut is also a First Aider and he's highly trained in dealing with minor medical emergencies. He even knew what to do when Goose twisted her neck during a music lesson once. To be honest, it had been completely her own fault because Mr Howells had already told her off twice for playing the guitar behind the back of her head.

Gareth stopped spluttering and muttered, 'Nah, I'm all right.'

I breathed a big sigh of relief and then I said, 'So do you want to borrow my concealer stick or what?'

Instantly, Gareth turned purple and started spluttering again.

'What's wrong?' I asked.

Taking a few deep breaths to calm himself, Gareth leaned back against the wall of the schoolyard, and then, after a shifty glance around to check that he couldn't be overheard, he said, 'Stop going on about that blinking . . .' He paused and dropped his voice even further, before adding uncomfortably, '. . . concealer thingy.'

'What's wrong with wearing a bit of cover-up?' I said. 'I've got some on now. It's heaps better than walking around with a snooker ball stuck to your chin.'

Gareth shot another edgy look around the schoolyard and said, 'Nothing's wrong with it *if you're a girl*. But you're not putting any of that stuff near my face because I'm blatantly a bloke. And blokes DON'T wear make-up.'

At this point I started laughing. Gareth is undeniably sweet and hunky and gorgeous but he's also ridiculously old-fashioned. During last year's unit on sexual reproduction, Mr Thomas, my double-science teacher, told us that all male mammals are made up of equal numbers of X and Y chromosomes. The X chromosome is the girly pleasant part and the Y chromosome is the magic ingredient which makes them grow extra dangly bits and causes their bedrooms to smell of woodland fust. Sometimes, though, it's difficult to believe that Gareth has got any of the X factor in him. He's definitely not in tune with his feminine side. If he was, he'd be begging to borrow my concealer stick.

'Why not?' I said, hurrying after Gareth who was stropping off in the direction of our form room with his hands in his pockets.

'Because . . .' said Gareth, with increasing annoyance, '. . . girls only wear it to impress boys anyway and—'

'NO WE DON'T,' I said, outraged. 'We wear it to please ourselves.' And then I added, 'Well, *I* do, because I'm a Type A person. All the women in my family are Type A people actually!' To be honest, I'm not sure if this is strictly true. My older sister Ruthie is away at university studying archaeology and I hardly ever see her wearing anything other than jeans and a muddy old parka. And my mum is a frumpy police woman.

Gareth stopped walking and looked confused. 'What the heck are you on about?' Before I could explain, he threw yet another shifty glance around the schoolyard, lowered his voice and added, 'Well, anyway, I don't wanna catch the Frillies!'

'The Frillies?' I said. 'What on *earth* is that?'

Just then, Gareth's friend, Spud, spun out from nowhere, jumped on top of Gareth's back and said, 'Someone giving

24

you an attack of the Frillies, Stingey?'

'YUCK NO!' said Gareth and threw Spud to the ground before punching him playfully in the head.

Spud returned the punch with a low biff to Gareth's stomach. He then swiped the remainder of Gareth's turkey sandwich from right out of Gareth's hand and ran off laughing. Until very recently, Spud and my friend Goose were in a relationship together. They are currently on a break because Goose has concerns that Spud might be too immature for her. She may have a point.

'Muppet!' grinned Gareth happily.

'What's the Frillies?' I demanded.

Gareth sighed and rolled his eyes. 'It's this weird girl disease we get if we hang around with girls too much. It's disgusting. It makes us become part girl.' Gareth shuddered. 'And it was a lot worse when we were little. We could get it then just from sitting *next* to a girl.' He shuddered again. 'And kissing one was a definite no-no.'

My mouth fell open in utter astonishment. 'Are you having a laugh?'

Gareth turned redder than the reddest red thing which has ever existed on the whole of the surface of Mars. For a second, I couldn't even see where his spot was any more because it had completely blended in with its red surroundings. With another embarrassed sigh, he said, 'I suppose we were being a bit childish back then. I can assure you that I'm completely OK about sitting next to girls now.'

'Well, hooray for that!' I said.

'But I still draw the line at make-up,' said Gareth firmly. And then he winked at me and said, 'I don't want to start an epidemic of the Frillies, do I?'

Before I could answer such a stupid question, he leaned in and gave me a great big Frilly-defying kiss, right there in the middle of the schoolyard. And, on instinct, I closed my eyes, wrapped my arms around him and instantly stopped worrying about anything as pointless and pathetic as a few random spots. To be honest, you don't even notice them when you've got your eyes closed.

When we'd finished kissing, Gareth's eyes lingered on mine and for a moment I was helplessly captivated in a highly romantic eye-lock. Without really knowing why, I held my breath – and when Gareth opened his mouth to speak, I just *knew* he'd say something that would perfectly capture the moment. In a weirdly wobbly voice, Gareth said, 'I love U2.' And then he coughed and started frowning down at his K-Swiss trainers and the romantic spell was broken.

'*What?*' I said.

'U2,' said Gareth, coughing again and clearing his throat. 'The rock band. I love their musical energy on stage and their commitment to serious world issues.'

'Oh,' I said, slightly confused. 'Thanks for sharing that fact with me.'

'No worries,' said Gareth, and then he took hold of my hand and we walked off to registration together.

Gareth is slightly odd sometimes. Gorgeous with it though.

NerD rash

If it seems totally tragic that I'm spending massive long chunks of my Friday night sitting alone in my bedroom and writing stuff on my computer, I should just explain that most of the time I have a very hectic social life. Last week, I went with Gareth to three sixteenth birthday parties in one evening and I also hung out at Goose's house for two whole days so that we could watch the entire first series of *Glee* on her new flat-screen 10-inch television. My school was closed for staff training so it's not as if we had anything else to do – apart from our science, maths and geography coursework, I suppose. We got as far as episode twenty but then my vision started going fuzzy and I had to go home. And even though I'm sitting typing all this stuff right now, I haven't been for long. I only got home an hour ago. To be honest, I'd expected some grief for being late without having cleared things with my mum first[4] but when I got back the house was all in darkness. I checked my phone and saw that my mum had actually sent *me* a text. It said:

> ### mum
>
> gone for a drink.
> won't be late.
> will bring home takeaway.
> love you x

---

[4] I was out of phone credit.

I was a bit shocked when I saw this. Texts of this nature are totally out of character for my mum because her life mostly revolves around catching criminals and watching television. In fact, she's a workaholic couch potato. My dad walked out when I was nine and I don't think she's ever fully recovered. To be fair though, it's not easy juggling a decent social life with a career in the police force. A lot of normal people find it hard to relax in the company of the long arm of the law. I'm one of them. Even so, I'm glad she's found some friends to go out with and I wish she wouldn't wait until it's practically Christmas Day before she lets herself lighten up.

On the subject of Christmas, one of my favourite things about it – apart from presents, school holidays and those skinny chocolate mints in their own individual envelopes – is that, all through December, the shops in the city stay open until late almost every night of the week. Even though I am seriously strapped for cash, I love riding in on the bus with Goose to look at the Christmas lights and to check out the latest clothes in the high street. And, luckily, Goose loves riding into town on the bus with me. Just recently, she's had enough money to buy bus tickets for both of us because she's got a new weekend job as an usherette in the Ponty-Carlo Picture House close to where I live. So we've been going into the city quite often and I massively prefer it to going home to an empty house and my mum's manky shepherd's pie.

And that's what we did after school today. We weren't the only ones. It seemed like half of my school was wedged on to the number 24 bus to the city centre. For a moment, I thought we'd have to stand up the whole way, but then Beca Bowen – who's in the same registration group as me – called us over and let us squeeze in next to her on the big long back seat. I was quite relieved because I'm not very good at balancing on buses. I think it's because I'm seriously short for my age and I can't actually reach the handrails, which are supposed to prevent you from pitching headfirst into someone's lap. So I gratefully sat down, wedged tightly between Goose and a skinny bloke I've seen in the sixth-form whose glasses had steamed over, and I felt all warm and happy and excited. There were so many people to look at and conversations to listen to that I almost didn't know what to focus on first.

And then I heard Goose ask, 'You going into town?'

I turned and looked at her confused. I think I'd been daydreaming for a second. 'Of course I am,' I said. 'You just bought me a ticket, remember!'

In a slightly irritated voice, Goose said, 'Sorry, Lotts, but I wasn't *actually* talking to you. I was talking to Tim.'

My confusion deepened. Next to me, the skinny sixth-former with the steamed-up glasses sat forward, cleared his throat and said, 'Yes, yes. It's time to confront that age-old dilemma of December – the conundrum that is the Christmas shopping.' He coughed nervously and looked down at his shoes. I did too. I was quite surprised by what I saw. Unlike everybody else on the bus whose feet were planted in trainers or soggy UGG boots, he was wearing *actual* proper shoes. And paisley-patterned socks pulled up very high over the ends of his beige cord trouser legs. He gave Goose a shy smile and added, 'My timing is regrettable though. I'm . . . er . . . feeling conspicuously *old* on here.' And then he made a funny little harrumphing noise which I think was supposed to be a laugh but sounded more like the noise a giraffe might make if it had a fly buzzing in its face.

To be honest, it's a wonder I can even remember anything that he said. My eyes were so amazed by some of his Type C styling decisions that my ears had stopped paying proper attention to what was coming out of his mouth.

Goose harrumphed back at him and said, 'I know. Helluva many kids on this bus. Most of this lot are only in Year 10.' And then she shook her head in utter disgust – as if being in Year 10 was the worst thing in the entire world. Even though we've only been in Year 11 since September.

Carefully, so that the square sixth-former couldn't see, I elbowed Goose in the ribs and pulled a face at her but she deliberately refused to look anywhere in my general direction. It's a pity because I think my face was doing something like this.

The bus rumbled on. Goose said, 'Are you working this weekend, Tim?'

Geeky Guy fiddled with a button on his duffel coat and said, 'Yes, yes. I'll be in the projection room in . . . um . . . precisely three hours from now. So . . . er . . . I'm afraid you're going to be stuck with me.' And then he made that giraffe noise again.

Goose, who had gone so red in the face that I thought she might be turning into a strawberry Starburst, said, 'Maybe we can talk about film noir again. It helps to pass the time, doesn't it?'

The way that Goose's voice got a bit louder at a certain point during that last sentence made me think that, just possibly, she had started to show off.

Square Boy frowned and then he said, 'Yes, yes.' And then, with another harrumph, he stood up and pressed the bell for the bus to stop.

Goose said, 'Oh! Are you going? I thought you were on your way to town?'

Freaky Bloke said, 'Yes, yes, but . . . er . . . um . . . first, there's a wonderful second-hand bookshop that I want to have a rummage around in.' And with one last final harrumph, he picked up his bag (a battered old leather briefcase), flashed Goose a twitchy smile and then lurched awkwardly down the aisle of the bus towards the stairwell.

As soon as he was out of sight, I grabbed Goose's arm and was just on the brink of demanding WHO ON EARTH he was when Beca Bowen – who has always had a bigger mouth than me – butted in first and said, 'HOLY COW CAKES! *WHO* IN DAME SHIRLEY BASSEY'S NAME WAS *THAT*???' And then Beca Bowen and I both started laughing our bras off.

Goose looked a bit fed up. 'He's just someone I work with.'

Beca Bowen said, 'No way! Does he bring you out in a nerd rash?' And she and I both cracked up laughing again. Thinking back on it now, I admit that there's a high probability that we were both acting like a couple of brainless bra-less numpties.

Whoops.

To be fair though, Beca Bowen was worse than me.

Goose's eyes flashed. 'He's *not* a nerd. He's just a bit different.' And then her cheeks flushed even redder than a blood-soaked strawberry Starburst wrapped up in a Chinese flag, and she added, 'Honestly, grow up! You two are being helluva childish.'

The driver made a sharp turn past the flickering fairy lights on the castle wall and everyone on the top deck sprang up from their seats. Goose and I pushed our way down the stairs and, once the bus had finally come to a halt, spilt out into the dark and drizzle. I shouted bye to Beca and waved as she crossed the street to join her friends in the burger bar on the corner. Goose didn't shout goodbye or wave. In fact, she'd already begun marching off in the direction of Maxi Style[5]

---

[5] Four floors of fashion at cost-cutting prices.

with her hands firmly in her pockets and a look of blatant aggravation fixed on her face.

I hurried after her. 'You're not *seriously* narked off because we were laughing at that Tim bloke, are you?'

'No,' said Goose.

'Doesn't seem like it,' I said.

Goose's eyes narrowed and so did her lips. Then she said, 'I just think you and Beca were being totally tight, that's all.' After another narrow-lipped pause, she added, 'And you of all people should know that it's not nice to laugh at someone just for being a bit different.'

The second that she said this, my face went boiling hot. I think my lips and eyes went a bit narrow as well. Anyone walking towards us would have seen this:

For a moment, I was annoyed with Goose because she had deliberately referred to something that I don't think should *ever* be casually referred to. Namely, how a few months ago, I got into really bad trouble with the police over some stolen shoes and then went so completely bananas that I had to see a doctor at the hospital. It was a very difficult time for me. When I was eventually well enough to go back to school, one or two people were quite horrible about it and called me names like nut-nut and schizo. One or two of them still do.

We walked on in silence for a bit and I started biting my thumbnail and thinking about how I'd laughed my bra off at the idea that Goose might come out in a nerd rash through working with somebody like that Tim bloke. To be honest, it didn't seem half as funny now that I didn't have Beca Bowen to laugh about it with me. Actually, it didn't seem funny at all.

'Point taken,' I muttered.

Goose shrugged. And then she smiled ever so slightly and said, 'It's OK. To be fair, I thought he was a bit nerdy too when I first met him. Honestly, Lottie, some of the jumpers he wears are horrendous. But he's all right, you know. I actually really like him.'

I stopped dead and stared at her. Before I could put my words through a Stupid Filter, I said, 'Oh my God, Goose! You *fancy* him?'

Goose stopped walking too and looked furious. 'YUCK! SHUT UP! I don't mean I like him like *that*! GET REAL!' And then she pulled a face something like the one I'd pulled on the bus and said, 'YOU ARE SO TOTALLY RIDONKULOUS SOMETIMES!'

'Ridonkulous?' I said.

'Yeah,' said Goose. 'TOTALLY AND UTTERLY RIDICULOUSLY RIDONKULOUS!' And then, to show me just how ridiculously ridonkulous I'd been, she pretended to chuck up into an invisible bucket. And when she'd finally finished blowing those air chunks, we both burst out laughing and hurried on towards Maxi Style to check out their wet-look shiny leggings.

DiLemmas aND CONuNDrums

When I got up this morning, my mum told me to write a Christmas list. She also told me that, in an hour or so from now, she's going to take me out to lunch and treat me to whatever I fancy from the menu. I said, 'Wow, take it easy, Mother! I might start to develop a brattitude.' And then I asked, 'What's the big occasion?'

My mum said, 'There isn't any big occasion. I'm feeling spontaneous. I can treat my little girl to lunch if I want to, can't I?' Then she pulled a stupid face at me and said, 'And, Lottie, you've had a brattitude for a while but when I'm wearing my brat shades, I don't notice it so much.' And then she took her sunglasses out of the kitchen drawer and put them on, even though we were indoors and it was the middle of winter.

'You are SO childish,' I said.

My mum pulled another stupid face and said in a stupid voice, 'Do I care though?' and then she started tickling me and wouldn't stop until I threatened to call *The Jeremy Kyle Show*.

It didn't stop her from annoying me though. By some weird trick of fate, the 'I Am What I Am' song started playing on the radio and my mum turned up the volume as high as it would go and began to sing along in a voice so ridonkulously loud that the neighbours could probably hear. The whole situation gave me such a severe case of cringe-flu that, for a second, I forgot where I was and thought I must be in a cringe-flu isolation ward at Cringetown General Hospital.

My mum is massively embarrassing sometimes.

She's also in a massively good mood at the moment. She doesn't even seem particularly bothered by the fact that horrible Detective Sergeant Giles keeps phoning her up at home when she isn't even supposed to be worrying her head about work. Nothing is getting her down. Her trip to the pub last night must have really done her some good. I can't help noticing that she's even started wearing a glamorous new shade of lipstick. It makes her look really nice and less like a fusty old policewoman.

Which is all well and good but I've still got some important issues to address.

Like my Christmas list.

The trouble is that, right now, I'm finding it really hard to stay focused on all that happy stuff. Because this time of year just brings me too many dilemmas. I've looked up the word *conundrum* in my dictionary. It says this:

conŭ'ndrum (noun) puzzle; difficult question

Goose's geeky friend was right. Christmas *is* a conundrum. Don't get me wrong – it's pure point-blank priceless quality, but it does throw up some very difficult and puzzling questions. Even deep-thinking philosophers like myself don't always have all the answers. I'm going to try and deal with them one at a time.

1. What do I *really* want to be given this year?

- a 9 inch flat-screen TV
- a Nintendog
- a poster of René Descartes
- a poster of Robert Pattinson
- a book called 'Philosophy for Beginners'
- a plug-in air-freshener
- purple leg warmers
- an orang-utan adoption pack
- a Santa hat for my chinchilla
- a laptop (<u>fat chance</u>!!)
- false eyelashes
- a beret (red or green)

I've thought about this long and hard. Here is my wish list. To be honest, I've got more chance of being elected as the next prime minister of Japan than I have of finding a TV or a laptop under our Christmas tree. My mum doesn't like the idea of me having a telly in my bedroom and she says that I don't actually need a laptop. But strictly speaking, apart from the false eyelashes, the leg warmers and the orang-utan adoption pack, I suppose I don't really *need* anything.

2. What am I going to give other people?

The only person I've asked so far is my mum. She said she'd

like the latest CD by Susan Boyle. I did my utmost then to steer her in the direction of the Kings of Leon or Lady Gaga but she wasn't having any of it. She said she quite liked Lady Gaga but she much preferred Susan Boyle's voice and appearance. I am now placed in a very awkward position. What if the person in the shop thinks I'm buying SuBo for myself???

3. How am I going to give them anything at all when I don't actually have any money?

This is sad but tragically true. Since I quit my last Saturday job of sweeping up stray human hairs in a hairdressing salon, the only income I have is the occasional bit of pocket money from my mum or dad whenever they take pity on me.[6] I don't like accepting their charity but, because I'm in no position to be proud and because they are my parents, I accept it anyway. Sometimes, when she's home, even my sister Ruthie gives me pocket money and she's a poverty-stricken student who survives on a diet consisting entirely of baked beans and bumper bags of jelly babies. I have no problem about taking money from her though because, if I didn't, she'd only waste her entire allowance on beer. Because this is what university students do.

4. As a follower of the philosophy of René Descartes,

---

[6] My dad lives in Wrexham which is three hours away by train. He doesn't like putting money in the post so I don't feel the financial benefit of his sympathy very often.

should I even bother to celebrate Christmas anyway? After all, the only thing that I can be truly certain of is my own existence.

It's not easy being a philosopher. There's a lot of thinking involved. I definitely think that we philosophers think more than most ordinary people think. But what's interesting is that if I added up all the time I've spent thinking about these first four conundrums, it still wouldn't come close to equalling the hours that I've spent worrying about the fifth and final one.

5. Who will I be spending Christmas Day with this year?

This might not seem like a tricky question to anybody else but it is to me and it's been niggling away at my brain for quite some time. The niggle started during an otherwise pleasant conversation in which Gareth asked me if I'd go to the end-of-term disco with him. It's just under a fortnight away and on the very last day of school. Everyone will be going. Even Candy Craddock in Year 10 – and she's got a mega-phobia of strobe lights. *I* love them though. And dry ice machines. I'd given Gareth a kiss and said, 'I certainly will, big boy,' and he'd looked all chuffed and added, 'Oh, and before I forget, my mum wants to know if you'll come and have your tea with us on Christmas Eve.' This time, instead of kissing him and calling him big boy, I got a bit flustered and started examining my split ends.

It's not that I don't want to have tea at his house. I do.

But the awkward truth is that I actually have no idea where I'll be on December 24th of this year. Or the 25th. Or the 26th. And this makes it very difficult for me to pre-arrange my personal life. It's OK for my older sister, Ruthie, because her life is much more straightforward than mine. Ruthie thinks that my dad's new wife, Sally, is a crusty hedge-pig. My dad and Sally know this and never invite her up to stay. But *I* get on OK with everyone and this just makes my life ridonkulously complicated. I'm a bit like the baton in a relay race. My mum gets to hold on to me for one Christmas and then the following year I'm passed up to Wrexham to spend Christmas with my dad and Sally and my little brother, Caradoc. And each year, I've been passed backwards and forwards like this since I was nine years old.

But now I'm not sure whose turn it is to carry the baton. Last year, Caradoc caught chickenpox and my dad phoned and cancelled my visit. I had to take my train ticket back to the railway station and they gave me a great big whopping refund because it's hideously expensive to go all the way from Cardiff to where my dad lives. After all, it's equivalent to the entire length of Wales. My dad let me keep the money so I went into town and bought myself some hot-pink hair-straighteners.[7] But I'd still have preferred to see my dad. And now it's practically a year later and my mum is talking about all the things we might do over the holidays and Gareth has

---

[7] Which was cool because I finally had hair that didn't look like beige candyfloss.

asked me to tea on Christmas Eve and Goose has invited me over to her house to watch *Glee* again and

I just don't know what to say.

Because I can't make any concrete plans as I'm sort of expecting my dad to invite me up north to spend the holidays with him. It's definitely his turn. And I know that he will invite me sooner or later.

He just hasn't yet.

Even Winnie can't help me with this one and Winnie is the Wisest Chinchilla in the Whole of Wales.

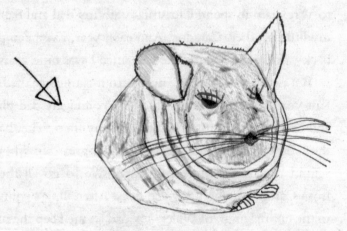

He's also extremely ancient and looks like a big scruffy snowball.

When I discuss my problems with Winnie, he makes a cute little chirping noise, twitches his ears a bit and falls asleep.

Winnie belongs to me even though he sleeps in Ruthie's room. He used to sleep in my room but he has this habit

42

of bouncing around all night and keeping me awake so, every evening, I relocate him down the hall. Ruthie is at university and hardly ever at home so she's not exactly in any position to complain.

I know it sounds weird but I often talk to Winnie and tell him my problems. Blake, my counsellor, says that it's perfectly normal to discuss important things with a pet and that pets are often the best counsellors of all. I agree. I know that Winnie listens to me because he has wise little eyes which watch me closely whenever I speak to him. And, considering that he's only a chinchilla, he's actually a remarkably good listener. I'd even say that he's as good at listening as Blake is – and Blake has probably had professional training. To be fair though, Blake is much better than Winnie at giving advice. Because Winnie can't speak. Obviously.

My mum can though. And she's just called up the stairs to tell me that it's time for us to go and get some lunch. Which means that the only conundrum I'm facing right now is what the hicketty-heck I'm going to eat. And that's not a very perplexing conundrum at all.

hOw I LearNeD that there's NO suCh thING as a free LuNCh

In school, I am forced to take Religious Education lessons. I don't understand why because I, personally, am not a particularly religious human person. I wouldn't say that I was an atheist though because atheists don't believe in God at all. And I do. I think. Otherwise, how could anyone as outrageously handsome as Robert Pattinson ever have been put on this earth for me to look at? [8]

But then again, belief in something as abstract as God conflicts with my basic philosophical principles. I asked my RE teacher, Mr Davies, about this only today and he actually gave me a helpful answer. I said, 'How can I believe in God when the only thing I can be absolutely certain of is my own existence?'

Mr Davies looked a bit surprised because he'd just been telling me to put my pickled onion crisps away and he pushed his glasses up his nose so that he could see me better. Then he rubbed his beard and said, 'Why do you say that?'

'Because Descartes said it,' I said.

Mr Davies looked even more surprised and then he said, 'Come again?'

I said, 'René Descartes, the father of modern philosophy, believed that we should question everything except the

---

[8] Unfortunately, only in posters. ☹

unquestionable. And the only unquestionable factor in all of this is that we are asking questions. And therefore we have a brain. And therefore we exist.' I sat back in my chair and felt a crisp crunch underneath me, and then added, 'But how do we know that God does?'

While I was saying all of this, I'd become aware that all of the other kids in my class were staring at me as if they'd just overheard me chatting in fluent French with the great philosopher himself. It made me smirk. I couldn't help it. I was feeling as tasty as a chocolate bar, to be honest.

Putting his two index fingers to his pursed lips, Mr Davies looked at me thoughtfully and then he said, 'I'm an RE man by trade, Lottie, so I tend to side with the more spiritual philosophers. Have you ever heard of Sir Francis Bacon?'

Instantly I stopped smirking and had to admit that, no, I hadn't.

Mr Davies scratched his ear and said, 'A *very* interesting man. *Very*. And a very *clever* man. Some people actually believe that it was Bacon who wrote the plays we associate today with the name of William Shakespeare. Yes they do. *Hmmm?* But the reason I'm bringing Bacon to the ideas table now, Lottie, is because he once said, *If a man will begin with certainties, he shall end in doubts; but if he will be content to begin with doubts, he shall end in certainties.*' And then Mr Davies put his index fingers back on his lips, nodded his head vigorously and said, 'Think about that! *Hmmm?* Think about that!'

I thought about it but I didn't get it. To be honest, I was

still trying to work out where the ideas table was. I rubbed my chin, pursed my lips and scratched my ear and finally said, 'So?'

Mr Davies pointed at me and, in a hushed voice, he said, 'You . . . are . . . unique! Think about that, Lottie. *Hmmm? Hmmm?* There is nobody else quite like you on this entire planet.' And then he looked around at the rest of the class and said, 'Every . . . single . . . one of you . . . is a totally . . . individual . . . and extraordinary . . . creation. *Hmmm?* Can we really be *certain* that God doesn't exist? Can we? *Hmmm?* Could anything as mundane and ordinary as mortal man really be solely responsible for populating the world with six . . . billion . . . walking . . . works . . . of art? *Hmmm? Hmmm?*'

Beca Bowen, who sits at the back of the class deliberately close to where there is a plug socket, put down her hair-straighteners and said, 'Yeah but, Davo, there's still no *hard evidence*, is there?'

Mr Davies shrugged and waggled his hands in the air and said, 'True, true . . . There will always be *doubts*. And I admit that a certain leap of faith is needed on this one but, then again, there's no such thing as a free lunch, is there? *Hmmm?* The world would be a very dull place otherwise, don't you think?'

And then he turned back to me and added, 'And what do *you* think, Lottie? Surely the fact that you exist is proof positive of some superior being, isn't it? *Hmmm?*'

I was a bit embarrassed then so I did my very best attempt

to impersonate Shrek and grunted, 'How the hicketty-heck should I know?' Secretly though, I was dead chuffed. Whichever way you look at it, Mr Davies had definitely paid me a very nice compliment. I'd never thought of myself as a walking work of art before.

And then Mr Davies carried on with the lesson and in it he talked about people who'd had near-death experiences and who had claimed to have seen bright white lights and dead relatives and their whole lives flashing in front of them at super high speeds, and then he made us write a list of the ten best moments we'd each experienced in our own lives and I chose the time that I got an A★ for my English coursework and the time Goose and me just sat thinking in my wardrobe and the time in the summer when Gareth asked me to go out with him and, after that, I got stuck because I couldn't actually think of any more. And then he asked us to think of a time that stuck out in our minds for all the wrong reasons and that was really easy because I've just lived through one of the worst weekends of my life. And the ironic thing is that it all started at the Hippo Eater *Happy* Pub.

The Hippo Eater Happy Pub is a gigantic bar and restaurant tucked neatly under the flyover on the very southern edge of Whitchurch village. No matter what the time of day or which day of the week it is, it's always incredibly busy and sometimes, when the population of Northern Cardiff is particularly hungry, the queue of people waiting for a table stretches right through the double front doors and spills out on to the big gravel car park. It was just like this on Saturday when my mum and I swung into one of the few remaining parking spots. There was no need for *us* to queue though because my mum had planned ahead and booked a table. Thinking back on it, I should have realized that this was the first telltale sign that my mum was not being spontaneous at all and was definitely and deliberately and deviously up to something.

I love the Hippo Eater Happy Pub. For a start, it's one of the few pubs that I've ever been in. Even though I'm in Year 11 – and am therefore easily old enough to be an under-age drinker – my experience of alcohol-vending establishments is pretty much limited to sipping soft drinks through a straw in the occasional fun-pub family area with my mum or dad. The truth is, that unlike some of the people in my year at school, I'd never dare to try and pass myself off as an eighteen-year-old because I'm really obviously only fifteen. And, unfortunately, from a certain angle in a certain light, I can tend to look about twelve. It's not particularly a problem though because I don't actually like alcohol. I tried some lager at a party once and it tasted so rancid that I'd seriously rather lick my own armpit.

But I do like pubs. I like the fact that they are quite dark and a bit noisy and the cola is extra sweet and slightly flat and comes in a glass with big cubes of ice and a slice of lemon. And I like the fact that it's totally illegal for my mum – who is, after all, a well-known policeperson – or dad to send me up to the bar with a ten-pound note to fetch all the drinks for them. Just for a change, I get to sit down and wait around like Lady Lazybones while they bring the drinks to me. And while I'm sitting there, I like watching the people crowding around the flashing quiz machines and cheering in front of the massive TV screens and leaning up against the bar and chatting each other up and laughing about secret things that I can't possibly hear because I'm tucked away in the safety of the family area.

And of the few pubs I've ever been inside, I like the Hippo Eater Happy Pub the most because they serve such a colossal choice of food that the menu is as thick as a telephone directory and the waiters and waitresses whizz around on roller skates and wear bright pink T-shirts which have I EAT LIKE A HAPPY HIPPO written right across the front. And I especially like the fact that the children's menu is only available to tweenies who are fourteen years old and under – which means that it's totally illegal for my mum to buy me anything from it and I'm actually fed like an adult for once.

But my mum hates the Hippo Eater Happy Pub. She hates everything about it. She hates the skating waiters; she hates their awful tacky T-shirts; she hates the big spongy seats; she hates the irritating quiz machines; she hates the unnecessarily extensive menu; she hates the obscene size of the portions; she hates the shocking amount of waste; she hates the anti-social presence of the gigantic flat-screen televisions; she hates the irresponsible promotion of greed. In short, my mum hates every single utter thing about the Hippo Eater. I know all this because every time we ever go there, she tells me. At length.

So I really should have guessed that my mum had a sneaky hidden agenda when she voluntarily whisked me away there for lunch.

But I didn't. Because I clearly wasn't thinking. And for a young Welsh philosopher like me, that was a very stupid oversight.

Things started going suspiciously weird-shaped within about three seconds of us passing through the main doors. Just as we arrived at the big desk with the sign that says . . .

Please wait for one of our Hippo Helpers to take you to your watering hole.

. . . Detective Sergeant Giles walked by us in his plain clothes. He did a dramatic double take, stared at my mum in amazement and then casually kissed her on the cheek. Just as if he was a French person or something. Immediately, I felt totally uncomfortable and started looking at my feet.

I heard Giles say to my mum, 'Carolyn! I never had you down as a hungry hippo kind of girl!'

My mum did this weird fluttery laugh I'd never heard her do before. It made her sound like she was having an asthma attack. Then she put her arm across my shoulders and said, 'I'm treating Lottie to lunch. It's about time we spent some time together and got up to date with each other's lives, isn't it, Lottie?'

Because I'd been forced into the conversation, I sort of looked at Giles and sort of looked at the floor and did one of those smiles which only involves moving your mouth. And then I said, 'Hmm.'

DS Giles said, 'Great minds think alike! I've just been enjoying a Hefty Hippo Swamp Burger with Lois,' and then he clapped his hand across the back of a girl about my age who was all dressed up like an emo.[9] She was very tall and had long straight hair which was beige on top and dyed jet black but just at the ends. She also had a pudgy face. Around her neck she was wearing this big spiky metal thing on a cord. I must have been looking at it for too long because she said, 'What are you staring at?'

DS Giles laughed and said to the scary emo girl, 'Show Lottie what they are.'

Scary Emo Girl tutted and looked annoyed, and then she lifted the spiky thing up and placed it over her eyes. She looked like this:

---

[9] Emotional Hardcore Punk – obviously! Even Cardiff has them.

'They're cyber-goggles,' she said.

'Wow!' said my mum. And then she said, 'Funky!' And immediately gave me another bout of cringe-flu.

'What's the point of them?' I asked.

Scary Emo Girl stared at me blankly from behind her spiky glasses and then she said, 'What's the point of you?'

DS Giles laughed again and said, 'Oh, you girls! I sense we've got some fun days ahead! Come on, Lois, let's leave Lottie and her mum to have their lunch.' And then he said, 'Carolyn, I'll call you!' And with that, he winked at my mum – bold as brass – and she blushed and said, 'Talk to you soon, Steve,' and then *Steve* and his horrible daughter left the building.

There are certain moments in my life where I get this

weird sensation which happens simultaneously in my brain and in my stomach. It's as if my brain sinks swiftly into my feet and my stomach rises rapidly up into my mouth. It only lasts for a couple of seconds but it's a very sickening experience. It's the sort of feeling I'd get if I finished an exam early and then realized, as I was walking out of the exam hall, that there were a whole load more questions on the other side of the paper. Or if I wrote a text which said YOUR BODY IS TOTALLY HOT and accidentally sent it to my dad instead of Gareth. I don't think there's an official name for this feeling but there flipping well should be. It was exactly what I was feeling right then.

I watched them leave and then I looked at my mum. She'd been watching them go as well and she had this weird faraway expression on her face.

Like this.

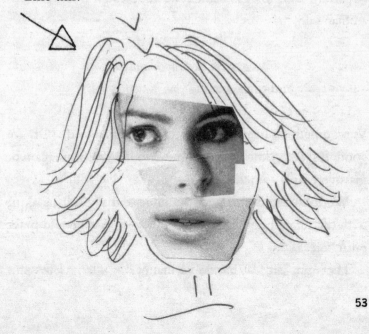

I didn't like the look in her eyes one bit. And all of a sudden, I was aware of a lot of worrying thoughts whirring around in my head and I couldn't quite get a grip on them and work out which thought was worrying me the most. Before I had a chance to regain control of my head, a person in a bright pink T-shirt said,

> *'My name is Sian – I'm your meeter-greeter.*
> *Thank you for choosing the Hippo Eater.'*

And then she said,

> *'Before you enjoy our marvellous cooking*
> *Please tell me which name you gave for your booking.'*

My mum said, 'Biggs. Table for two, please.'
Sian said,

> *'OK guys, let's rock and roll.*
> *Please follow me to your watering hole.'*

Very quietly, under her breath, my mum said, 'Oh for goodness sake, knock it on the head!' My mum can be massively rude sometimes.

We followed Sian over to a table and she left us alone with the telephone directory menus so that we could make our choices.

My mum said, 'What do you fancy?'

I pushed aside my Happy Hippo Christmas Cracker and opened up the menu. For all I cared, it may as well have been written in Morse code by someone wearing cyber-goggles. Because I didn't fancy eating anything.

My mum said, 'How about a Double Hippo Club Burger?'

I shook my head.

My mum said, 'A Happy Hippo Hot Pot?'

I shook my head.

My mum said, 'An All-Day Hungry Hippo Breakfast?'

I said, 'What did Giles mean when he said *I sense fun days ahead*?'

Without looking up from her menu, my mum said, '*Steve*. His name is Steve. Don't call him by his surname, Lottie; it's not polite.'

I said, 'What did *Steven* mean when he said *I sense fun days ahead*?'

At that moment, Sian returned and said,

*'I don't wish to hurry you or appear at all rude
But are you ready to order your food?'*

My mum said, 'No. Can you give us another couple of minutes, please?'

Sian skated off again.

I said, 'There's something weird going on.'

My mum put down her menu and said, 'Lottie, there's nothing remotely weird going on.' And then she sighed and said, 'We do need a chat though.'

'I knew it!' I said.

My mum gave me a very long and penetrating look and then she said, 'I don't know if you've noticed but I've been feeling really very happy just recently.'

Even though she paused, I knew there was more that my mum wanted to say. But suddenly, I really wasn't very sure if I actually wanted to hear it. Feeling breathless and panicky, I gripped hold of the edge of the table and said, 'Why did *Steven* wink at you?'

My mum has this pointless problem with elbows on dining tables. For some reason that has never been fully explained to me, she thinks that resting your elbows on the table is a shocking sign of colossal rudeness. So when she put her own elbows on the table and rested her forehead in the palms of her hands, I did consider telling her to remember her manners. I only considered it though. I don't have a death wish. After what felt like thirty years, she said, 'I've been feeling really happy just recently, and—'

Sian skated up from behind her and said again,

'I don't wish to hurry you or appear at all rude
But are you ready to order your food?'

In a blatantly irritated voice, my mum said, 'We'll both have a Hot Pot.'

Sian said,

'Please allow me to clarify
To save your order from going awry;
two Happy Hippo Hot Pots?'

'Yes,' said my mum.

Sian beamed and skated off towards the kitchens.

'Did I say I want a Hot Pot?' I said. 'Because I don't.'

My mum squeezed her temples as if she was trying to decide whether her head was ripe for eating or not and then said, 'Lottie, you're making this really difficult for me.'

'Making what difficult?' I said. I said it a bit louder than I meant to. Even though I didn't have a clue what was going on, I could tell that there was something very bad lurking just around the corner and it was putting me in an extremely edgy mood. If you must know, I had more edge than the entire coastline of the African continent and according to my geography teacher that has 356,000 kilometres of edge.

'Lottie,' said my mum. 'Can we talk like adults?'

I felt sick.

My mum said, 'I'm your mother. I'll always be your mother. But I'm a woman too and I've been on my own a long time and—'

'You're not on your own,' I said. 'You've got me and Ruthie.'

'Yes, I know,' said my mum. 'But Ruthie has also got Michel and you've also got Gareth.'

Michel is my sister Ruthie's boyfriend. They study

archaeology together at Aberystwyth University. It's quite sweet when you think about it. They found each other through their shared love of broken pottery and old pterodactyl bones. He's a bit boring but he's OK.

The reason why he's got a girl's name is because he's French.

My mum said, 'Are you listening?'

I nodded. Without realizing it, I'd started to rip the paper Hippo Eater Slop Mats into hundreds of tiny pieces.

'Well,' continued my mum. '*I* need a special friend too. And I'm happy to say that I think I've found one. And he's a really nice man.'

I didn't say anything. I couldn't. My jaw had frozen.

A plate of Happy Hippo Hot Pot was suddenly whacked down on the table in front of me. Sian said,

'Give me a shout if you need more grub,
And enjoy your meal in our Hippo Eater Pub.'

And then she skated off again. To be honest, I was starting to understand why my mum hates the Hippo Eater so much. After about two seconds, it's a seriously annoying place. I took a deep breath and said, 'Please don't tell me that you're having an affair with Giles!'

My mum said, 'I'm not having an affair! And neither is he. We're both free agents.'

I looked at my Hot Pot and fought back the urge to be sick over it. I was suddenly feeling iller than the illest person in the whole of Illinois. I didn't want to hear my mum using phrases like *free agent* and *special friend*. It was plain wrong!

'*Detective Sergeant Giles!*' I said, almost gagging on my own vom. '*You are joking?*' I think I might have been crying at this point.

'He's called Steve,' my mum said quietly.

'I don't care whether he's called Starvin' Marvin or Marvin Luther King – you still shouldn't be going out with him!'

'Mar*tin* Luther King,' my mum said. 'Not Marvin. And I think you're being very unfair. You don't even *know* Steve and, anyway, you can't tell me who I can or cannot go out with.'

'No! YOU'RE the one being unfair,' I said. 'Of all the people in all the world, YOU have to choose THE ONLY ONE who has ever cautioned me for being a shoe thief! How am I supposed to be OK with that?'

While I'd been saying all of this, some part of my brain was telling me to keep my voice down because there were people on other tables who were blatantly turning round to have a gawp. But I couldn't keep my voice down. I was really wound up.

My mum said, 'Keep your voice down, please. There are people looking at us.'

Even though I knew she was totally right, I said, 'Do I actually care though?'

Through clenched teeth, my mum said, 'You are being SO childish!'

I said, 'No I'm not. YOU'RE the one who is acting all weird and talking about SPECIAL FRIENDS. You've even changed your lipstick just to impress Stevie Wonder. That's WELL PATHETIC! I used to respect you but now I can see that you're nothing but a SAD and TRAGIC Type B person!'

My mum pushed her Hot Pot away from her and said, 'I've got no idea what you are talking about now. But you're causing a scene. Put your coat on. We're leaving.'

Tears were swimming across my eyes and causing my vision to go all fuzzy. I didn't want to be having this hideous row with my mum but, for some reason, I just didn't seem to be able to stop myself. It's like I was being operated from afar by a psychopath with a remote control. Without moving I said, 'But why *him*, Mum? Why did you have to go and pick the only policeman in the whole of South Wales who has got me under closed-circuit surveillance?'

And then my mum raised her voice too and said, 'Oh for God's sake, Lottie, you're just being absolutely absurd!' And before I even knew what was happening, she'd put some money on the table, picked up her coat and was saying, 'I can't sit here any longer. I honestly can't. I'll be in the car.'

And she went.

My head had gone completely blank. I sat all alone at the table and tried to get a grip on myself. Remembering a technique that Blake, my counsellor, once taught me, I closed my eyes and breathed slowly and deeply.

In and out.
In and out.

After a minute or so of doing this, I felt the pressure ease in my body and it suddenly seemed a lot less likely that my heart was going to crash its way right through my ribcage.

Next to me, someone noisily cleared their throat.

I opened one eye.

It was Sian, the waitress. She said, 'You know what, I can't be arsed with all this rhyming crap right now. I just wanted to check you're all right.' Then she said, 'Is there anything I can do?'

I opened up the other eye too and looked at her properly. I was still crying. 'I doubt it,' I said very quietly, between gulps for air. And then I shrugged and said, 'Unless you want to adopt me?'

Sian shook her head and smiled at me. 'Not really, to be honest.'

I nodded sadly and smiled back but it was another one of those smiles that only involves moving the mouth. 'I don't blame you,' I said. And then I put on my coat and went outside to find my mum who I knew would still be sitting in her car waiting for me.

hOw Me aND MY Mum wrOte Letters

We drove home in silence. When we got back to the house, I stormed straight up to my bedroom and sat down inside my wardrobe. I'm well aware that this makes me sound like a bunch of bananas but it's actually totally OK because I don't tend to view it as a wardrobe. I view it as more of a Think Tank. With clothes in.

I sat in there for quite a while and even though my body wasn't moving at all, my inner being was moving about massively. It was going on a journey.

At the start of that journey, my inner being was doing this:

And the words it was screaming at me were these:

DETECTIVE SERGEANT GILES

SPECIAL FRIEND I'm a woman too

really nice man FREE AGENT

we must stop meeting like this
Stevie Wonder Oh,

I sense fun days ahead

YOU'RE BEING

ABSOLUTELY

ABSURD

But it takes a lot of intensive energy to keep up this level of brain activity and after some time sitting there in the dark, freaking out at a thousand miles per minute, my inner being must have got quite knackered because, gradually, I started to calm down. And pretty soon, I felt less like a skull in a hoody and slightly more like an emotional hardcore punk.

And this time, instead of screaming at me, my inner being was just mumbling and muttering to itself. And the words that it was mumbling and muttering were these:

> you're being absolutely absurd you're being absolutely absurd
> you're being absolutely absurd

And within a short while, I started to feel less like an emotional hardcore punk and more like the biggest nerd in the entire nerdiverse. Because it began to occur to me that possibly – just possibly – my mum was right and I *was* absurd. I clambered out of my wardrobe and sat on my bed for a bit and then I got up and took my dictionary off my bookshelf and looked up the word *absurd*.[10] It said this:

absur´d *adjective* silly; ridiculous; incongruous

And even though I didn't have a flipping clue what incongruous meant, I understood the words *silly* and *ridiculous* perfectly well and I'm still troubled by those words even now and it doesn't make me feel very clever when I think that possibly – just possibly – this is how I've been behaving. So then I looked up the word *incongruous* and it said this:

incŏ´ngruous *adjective* absurd; out of place; disagreeing

---

[10] Don't get me wrong, I *know* what this word means. But there are certain times in life when you need a *precise* definition and only a dictionary can provide it. Otherwise, you just carry on remaining all discombobulated.

I put down the dictionary and scratched my head. However much I wanted to deny it then, and would still like to deny it now, I have to admit that the Hippo Eater Happy Pub is really not the place to throw a wobbler. Some people might even argue that my behaviour in the Hippo Eater at Saturday lunchtime was actually downright disagreeable and the mark of someone with a totally bad brattitude.

I scratched my head again and put the dictionary back on the shelf. Then I did what I always do when I need an immediate honest answer to an important direct question. I picked up my phone and texted Goose.

> **do u think i'm absurd???**

And barely a minute later, my phone bleeped back at me with Goose's reply.

> **goose**
>
> so wot if u r?
> life is absurd!
> ☺

Which made me feel ever so slightly better but only by a microscopic mini-fraction. To be honest, with each passing second, I was getting more and more and more regretful about having told my mum that she was sad and tragic.

I switched off my mobile and stared into space. I was beginning to feel quite sad and tragic myself. Blake, my counsellor, once told me that when I'm feeling like this, it's probably best not to think too much. He reckons I should try to switch my head off and allow myself to float quietly through the dreary feeling. Then, when I'm feeling more positive and in control of things, I can do all the thinking and reflecting I need in order to avoid the same situation happening again.

So I switched my head off and tried to think of nothing.

Downstairs, the sound of the telephone cut through the silence. I curled up on my bed and put my pillow over my head and continued trying to think of nothing. It's a surprisingly difficult thing to do. Instead of thinking of:

I was now thinking about how it was really warm and cosy under my pillow and how it smelt faintly of hair dye. And

I was also thinking about how I could still hear the stupid blinking telephone. Which led me to thinking about how my mum obviously wasn't in any sort of mood to pick it up.

After a few more noisy and thought-packed seconds, the answer-machine finally kicked into operation and the house plunged back into silence. I took the pillow away from my face and sat up again. On the opposite wall of my bedroom, a picture I had of René Descartes which I'd printed off the internet stared back at me. Underneath I had scribbled the words:

I think therefore I am!

And when I read those words again, it suddenly dawned on me that, in spite of all Blake's good advice, I needed to listen to what the father of modern philosophy was telling me and actually start thinking straight away. Because, somehow, I had to make things better between me and my mum.

And seeing as how I'm much better at writing than I am at thinking, I got up from my bed, picked up a notepad and pen from my desk and decided to write down exactly what was in my head and why I was feeling so completely cheddarly-cheesed off.

Before I even knew what was going on, I had written my mum a letter. It went like this:

Dear Mum

I apologize if my behaviour in the Hippo Eater was absurd
and incongruous. The truth is that I'm finding it very difficult
to get my head around the fact that you are 'special
friends' with Detective Sergeant Giles (Steven) and,
right now, I feel extremely discombobulated. However, I
understand that you are a woman with womanly needs and
not just my mother and I understand too that you are a
free agent so it's completely up to you who you choose to
get up close and personal with. So I promise I will do my
best to adapt to this present difficult situation. However,
I'd be lying if I said I was cool with it because I'm not.
I'm actually about as _cool_ as I would be if I was wearing
fluffy thermal pyjamas on a particularly hot day on the
surface of the sun.

I'd even go so far as to say that this situation has made
me miserable.

But please don't let that stop you from having a relationship
with Steven.

Yours sincerely,
Lottie.

I read it through a couple of times. It said what needed to be
said. I put the letter in the pocket of my jeans, opened my

bedroom door and listened. The house was still really quiet. Weirdly quiet. I couldn't hear any of the usual Saturday sounds. Sounds like the TV or my mum singing along to the radio or the thump thump thump of her jumping around to her fitness CD. I snuck along the landing to my mum's room and knocked nervously on the door. There was no answer so I pushed the door open to check that she wasn't hiding from me and then I went to Ruthie's room and pushed that door open too. Inside, Winnie was sitting up and washing his little white face. It's extremely rare for Winnie to be awake before teatime so I took this as a sign that he wanted to give me some moral support, scooped him up and carried him along with me. At the bottom of the stairs, I paused again and listened. There was really no sound at all. Nothing.

Puzzled, I wondered for a second if my mum was doing something in the garden but then I saw the rain hammering against the hallway window and decided that this was probably unlikely.

Shifting Winnie to my other arm, I crossed over to the telephone table which stands in a corner of our hallway and pressed the button on the answer machine. After three short beeps, Gareth's voice broke the silence.

'Hey Lottie, Gareth it is. I was just wondering if you wanted to come and see a film with me tonight. *Love, Lies and Secrets* is on at the Ponty-Carlo. It's supposed to be one of those romcom things. Not my type of film if I'm honest but I thought *you* might like it. Ring me back, yeah.'

Even though I wasn't in the mood for smiling, I smiled anyway. I couldn't stop myself. Normally, Gareth only ever likes to watch films about Rocky Balboa or rugby. Hanging around with me must be seriously giving him the Frillies.

Minutes later, I saw the note. It was in the kitchen, pinned up on the door of the fridge with a magnet. There was nothing weird about that. My mum and I often use the fridge door as a message board. What was unusual, though, was the length of the note. Usually our messages say things like *Your shepherd's pie is in the microwave* or *I'm at Goose's*. But this new note was abnormally long. Still clutching Winnie, I took it off the fridge and read it. It said this:

Lottie,

I'm sorry that lunch worked out so badly. It was really very unfortunate that we ran into Steve before I'd had the opportunity to explain to you how things have developed between him and me. He certainly didn't help make things any easier; no wonder you were freaked out!

I hope though, that when you've had a chance to calm down and think things through, you'll feel less terrible about all this. Although I've worked in the same building as Steve for years, it's only recently that we've got to know each other and we get on so well and have so much in common that it can hardly be a bad thing.

So how about giving me a break?

I could certainly do with one. Even though I'm as tough as old boots and have single-handedly reduced crime in the Cardiff area by about 200%, I still have feelings and some of the things you said to me today were very hurtful and upsetting.

I'm having a cup of tea next door if you need me.

Mum

And even though I had Winnie's warm little body cuddled up tightly right next to mine, I was suddenly overcome by this massive landslide of loneliness. I was the loneliest person in the entire loneliverse. Sort of like this:

For a moment, I just stood there, floating without a radio in space, and stroked Winnie's warm little head. Then, carefully, I put him down on the floor. Taking my own letter out of my pocket, I unfolded it and read it through again. And then I scrunched it up into a tiny ball and buried it in the rubbish bin where my mum would never see it. Because I'd suddenly got this feeling that it *didn't* say what was needed, after all. Taking a pen from the kitchen drawer, I turned over my mum's note and wrote a single word on the back of it.

SORRY.

And then I stuck it back on the fridge and hoped from the very bottom of my heart that my mum would never again feel the need to write me a letter and run away to have a cup of tea with the next-door neighbour. I hadn't even heard her leave. But I suppose this is one of the dangers of sitting inside a wardrobe or burying your head under a pillow.

hOw we Came tO aN UNCOmfOrtaBLe arraNGemeNt

Since then we've spent the last forty-eight hours giving each other lots of space. Our house currently has more space in it than the entire solar system. Today, I got home from school at seventeen minutes past four and it's now forty-three minutes past nine and I've pretty much spent every three hundred and twenty-six of those intervening minutes up here in my bedroom with the door closed. I've managed to get tons of stuff done though. I've done all of my history homework, written down heaps more of my random reflections and philosophical thoughts and joined eighty-seven different groups on Facebook – including:

I WAS FORCED TO LEARN THE RECORDER AS A CHILD.

1829 Members

JOIN

FRESH PRINCE OF BEL-AIR

WE KNOW THE ENTIRE FRESH PRINCE OF BEL-AIR 'RAP'.

102 Members

JOIN

MY GCSEs ARE SLOWLY KILLING ME.

24,763 Members

JOIN

I'M WELSH AND I LOVES IT.

84 members

JOIN

I can't remember what the other eighty-three are.

But obviously, I haven't been shut up in here for *all* that time. Occasionally I've popped down the hallway to check up on Winnie and I've visited the bathroom three times and I did also go downstairs for a while and eat tea with my mum but the conversation between us was unnaturally flat and lacked its usual sparkle. My mum asked me how my day had been and I said it was pretty much like most other Mondays and then we had a conversation about the sausages we were eating and how they tasted much nicer than the usual brand we buy but how, actually, they cost a staggering twelve pence less. Ordinarily, this is not the kind of thing that my mum and I would bother to discuss.

But nothing is very ordinary at the moment.

In fact, it's all gone a bit pear-shaped, wonk-ways and completely downside-up. I don't know how to behave around my mum and I get the distinct impression that she isn't exactly sure how to behave around me either.

On Saturday, after I found her note on the fridge, I went into the living room and flopped out in front of the TV. To be honest, I just put it on so that I could hear some other human voices. But then, because every human voice on the television was talking total drivel and irritating my bits off, I ended up switching over to the Welsh language channel. This was actually a lot less irritating because I no longer had the foggiest clue whether anyone was talking total drivel or not. On the screen, a young guy wearing a pin-striped suit was playing a purple guitar and singing to an audience of old folks in an old folks' home. The titles on the screen told me that his name was Harri Parry and his song was called *Lladfa yn y Disgo*.[11] Even though I couldn't understand a single word that he was singing, he had quite a nice voice and was strumming a very relaxing tune. Throughout the whole song, the old folks sat with their heads down, blatantly asleep, but when it was over they all jumped up in their seats and started clapping and wolf-whistling and banging their walking-frames on the floor. Then they threw their cushions at him. It was classic! I'm definitely going to try to watch Welsh telly a bit more often.

I don't think Winnie liked it much though. As soon as the song began, he ran off and hid behind the back of the sofa, leaving me all on my own. So when it had finished and the programme had moved on to an interview with a man who was shovelling piles of poo out of a pigsty, I pressed the mute button to encourage Winnie to come out from his hiding-place and sit with me again. But he wouldn't. In the corner of the living room, the lights on our Christmas tree were twinkling and changing colour and, after a while of watching them, I struggled up from the sofa and switched them off. And then, because I was in a bit of a dark mood, I turned off the living room lamp as well so that the only light in the room was the flickering light of the silenced television.

---

[11] Gareth knows more Welsh than I do so I asked him to translate this for me and he said it means 'Carnage at the Disco'.

An hour or more must have passed like this before finally, I heard the noises I'd been waiting for. The front door creaked open and then slammed shut and my mum's footsteps moved towards the kitchen. I heard the click of the light switch and then there was a moment of silence which, to me, seemed noisier than all the other stuff put together. This was replaced by the sound of my mum's footsteps again, and the door of the living room was pushed open. My mum was holding the fridge-note in her hand. Without looking at me, she walked over to the TV and switched it off and then she crossed over to the lamp and switched it on, before moving over to the Christmas tree and switching those lights on as well. Then she turned around and jumped right out of her skin.

'Hi,' I said.

My mum said, 'Why on earth are you sitting in the dark?'

'Sorry. I didn't mean to make you jump.'

My mum looked at me. She had a very serious expression on her face. It was the most serious expression I'd seen on her face for ages. Even her glamorous new shade of lipstick didn't do anything to soften the overall effect of deadly seriousness. After a second or so of total tension, she said, 'Never mind that – how about a proper apology for the way you talked to me this lunchtime!' And then she held up the piece of paper taken from the fridge door.

'That *is* a proper apology,' I said.

My mum gave me another long hard serious stare and then, finally, she sat down on the chair opposite me and said,

'You really upset me, you know.'

I sat with my head down, just like I'd seen the old folks on the TV doing earlier. I was blatantly wide awake though.

My mum said, 'I've been on my own for six years, Lottie. Six years! Is it really so impossible for you to be happy for me now?'

'Sorry,' I said.

My mum sniffed.

I chewed my thumbnail for a moment and then I said, 'I'm not going to find him sneaking around our house in a dressing gown, am I? Because that would really freak me out.'

My mum looked shocked. 'We've only just started seeing each other. What kind of a woman do you think I am?'

I smiled a bit then. My mum smiled a bit too. 'Sorry,' I said again, louder this time.

'Apology accepted,' said my mum.

And then, because it had been on my mind, I said, 'Gareth phoned up earlier and invited me to go to the cinema with him tonight. Can I go or am I grounded?'

My mum raised her eyebrows. 'Am *I* grounded?'

'Huh?' I could hardly believe my own ears. My mum was actually asking *me* if *she* was grounded! Confused, I searched her face to see if she was joking. She wasn't.

'Well,' explained my mum, 'I don't see why *you* should get to go out but *I* have to sit in the house all by myself on a Saturday evening. That doesn't seem very fair to me.'

I sighed. She's a very clever woman, my mum. It's hardly surprising that she manages to out-manoeuvre all those shifty Cardiff criminals. Through gritted teeth, I said, 'If you want to go out tonight with Stevie Wonder, that's perfectly fine by me.'

'Smashing!' said my mum. 'So the arrangements for this evening are settled.' And then, for the second time that afternoon, she jumped right out of her skin because Winnie picked that exact moment to come out from behind the sofa and bounce straight into her lap.

hOw MICheLaNGeLO stOPPeD me BehavING LIke a tOtaL turNIP

On the stroke of seven o'clock, Gareth rang the front doorbell. Gareth is a very punctual person. I've never once known him to be late. But what's unusual about Gareth is that I've never known him to be early either. As I opened the door, I said, 'How do you do it, Gaz? Bang on seven! Your timekeeping is *extreme*!'

Gareth kissed me on the lips for five full seconds and when he'd finished he said, 'Extreme's got nothing to do with it, Lottie Biggs. I'm just in control of the situation, that's all.' Then he drop-kicked an invisible rugby ball through an invisible pair of goalposts at the end of our hallway and added, 'Wanna know what Coach Jenkins has to say on the subject?'

'Of course!' I said, my eyes round with exaggerated eagerness. 'I'd be extremely interested to know.' And then I smiled very sweetly. Gareth thinks that Coach Jenkins is the man with the plan. Coach Jenkins is in charge of the school rugby team and Gareth goes on about him quite a lot.

Gareth looked at me disapprovingly and waved his finger in my face. 'I hope you're not being disrespectful to The Jenkins, young lady, cos he's the chief with the beef.' I waited. I knew there was more to come. Sure enough, Gareth bunched his fist into an imaginary microphone, raised it to his mouth and made a few random beatbox noises.

Then, while working the decks of a non-existent turntable, he sang, 'He's the geezer with the visa – he's the dude in the snood – he's the okey-doke bloke with the masterstroke!' And then he started beatboxing again.

I'd never seen him do this before. It made me giggle.

Gareth grinned and said, 'To be honest, it works better when me and Spud do it as a freestyling dubstepping duo.' And then, nodding his head thoughtfully, he added, 'But in all seriousness, Coach Jenkins reckons that time flies and if we aren't careful pilots, we'll end up as mutilated victims in the twisted wreck of the air crash.'

'Wow,' I said. 'That's cheerful!'

Gareth shrugged. 'Coach Jenkins says a lot of things and not all of them are cheerful. Coach Jenkins reckons that sometimes you gotta be blunt to stay in front.'

I don't know whether it was the sublime rhyme in his concise advice or whether it was the influence of the street coming up through his feet but, whatever it was, Gareth started to beatbox again. At the same time, my mum stuck her head into the hall and said, 'Hi, Gareth.' Instantly, Gareth stopped beatboxing, turned as red as the dragon on the Welsh flag and mumbled, ''lo, Mrs Biggs.' Then he lapsed into an embarrassed silence.

My mum said, 'Have a nice time, you two.' And then, for the first time since our disastrous lunch, she grinned. 'And I love those block-rocking beat noises that you were just making, Gareth. Very funky.'

Gareth's face went even redder than the dragon on the

Welsh flag. Mine probably did as well. I think it's safe to say that we were both fighting off a really nasty attack of the cringe-flu. My mum turned to me and said, 'Be back by eleven.'

'You too,' I said a bit sharply.

'I will be,' said my mum a little sharply back to me. 'But have you got your key, just in case?'

I hooked my door key out of my pocket and swung it around on my little finger to show her.

My mum nodded. 'OK. Well, make sure you don't lose it.'

'You too,' I said.

'And don't get into any trouble,' said my mum.

'You too,' I said.

My mum frowned and, just for a second, the horribly serious expression that I'd seen on her face earlier reappeared. She widened her eyes, flared her nostrils and tilted back her head to glare at me. Sort of like this:

---

[12] This is one of the animals that sits on the wall of Cardiff Castle in the centre of town. There are bears and monkeys and all sorts of things sitting on that wall – but sadly no chinchillas or orang-utans.

If anything, the glamorous new shade of red lipstick actually made her look a little meaner. But then, just as I was starting to feel really edgy, she did a big syrupy over-smiley smile and said, 'And make sure you have a lovely time!'

'Mmm,' I said and picking up my bag, I hurried Gareth through the door.

Once we were safely outside, Gareth said, 'What was all that about?'

'What was what about?' I asked.

Gareth wrinkled up his nose. 'All that woman tension. The atmosphere in there was horrible.'

I wrinkled up my own nose and said, 'My mum's got a new boyfriend.' In this context, the word *boyfriend* sounded really wrong coming from my mouth. Plain wrong. It *felt* wrong too. It was like saying something dodgy like *breaststroke* or *cockroach*. I didn't like it.

'So?' said Gareth.

'So!' I said. 'So! So it's only the exact same bloke who cautioned me after that whole shoe shop catastrophe!'

'Oh,' said Gareth. And then he said, 'So?'

I stopped walking and looked at him in disbelief. 'So!' I said. 'So! So I've already got one uptight law-enforcer in my face. I don't need another one, thank you very much. It'll be like living inside an episode of *The Bill*.'

Gareth shrugged and put his arm around me. 'So what's he said to you then?'

'Well . . .' I said, slightly surprised by the question. 'Nothing yet. But he's bound to say something sly, isn't he?'

'Is he? I doubt it.' Gareth let his arm fall and looked puzzled. We'd slowed to a stop and tiny flakes of snow I'd not even noticed falling began to settle on our clothes, making us look like the BEFORE photo on a dandruff advertisement. Gareth shivered and added, 'He's hardly going to give you a hard time if he wants to impress your mum.'

'It's easy for you to say,' I said. 'You're not the one who has to put up with him sniffing around.'

Gareth adjusted his scarf so that it was covering his ears. He'd come out without a coat on and I think he was regretting it. He does *own* a coat but he tends not to wear it because he reckons that it makes him look like the chubby bloke out of Take That. Wrapping his arms tightly around himself, he said, 'I'm not being funny, Lottie, but the crux of the matter is that at the end of the day when all's said and done, it's not exactly *you* he's sniffing around, is it? It's your mum.'

'Urggghhhh,' I said. 'Don't be tasteless!'

Gareth flapped his elbows and blew a flake of snow off the end of his nose. Then he shivered again and said, 'I say what I see, babe. And it's not Coach Jenkins speaking now, it's Gareth David Lloyd George Stingecombe. And from where I stand, I don't see what the problem is. So chill out a bit, babe.' He stamped his feet impatiently on the pavement. 'Now, are you coming or what?'

I stood there,

completely stunned.

Gareth said, 'It's nippy noodles standing here and I'm getting soaked. So I'll see you there, shall I?' And with that, he began walking down the street without me.

For a moment, I remained where I was, frozen to the pavement, watching him walk further and further ahead. But then, just as soon as I'd got to grips with the astonishing and impressive revelation that Gareth has not one but three middle names, I made a mental note to chill out and hurried through the darkness and snow to catch him up.

The Ponty-Carlo Picture House is one of my favourite places in the whole world. As cinemas go, it's not immediately obvious why I love it so much. I don't think I can even explain it properly myself. The whole place stinks like a school gym and the films that are on offer have been knocking about for so long that we've usually already seen them on pirate DVD. In the foyer, a scary old woman with peroxide hair sells us crumbly chocolate bars, which are a month or two past their sell-by date, and bucket-sized cups of unspecified cola. Whatever that cola is, it definitely isn't Coke and it definitely isn't Pepsi either. Everyone calls the old woman Pat Mumble because her name is Pat and she mumbles, and everyone says her teeth are wooden because they are brown and her breath smells of furniture polish. But so long as we give her the right change and say *please* and *thank you*, I don't think she actually cares. And we all do say *please* and *thank you* to Pat Mumble because otherwise she comes out from behind her sweet counter and has a massive mumbling go at us.

But we all love the Ponty-Carlo regardless. For a start,

it's fantastically cheap. In fact, it's the cheapest cinema in the whole of Wales. I know this for a fact because on the wall outside there is a massive orange poster that says:

**The Ponty-Carlo
Picture House
The cheapest cinema in
the whole of Wale's**

Mr Wood, my English teacher, told our class that he used to pass this poster every day on his way to school but now he deliberately takes another route. He says his doctor told him he had to because each time he saw that 'absurd apostrophe' it gave him chest pains. To be honest, Mr Wood could do with chilling out a bit as well.

But another reason that we all love the Ponty is because it's *ours*. Unlike the massive multi-screen complexes that keep sprouting up around the city centre and down the Bay, no one goes to the Ponty other than the people who live within a half-mile radius of it. Nobody else would want to. But *we* do because it's just at the end of our high street and, like I said, it's as cheap as chips. And, to be honest, there isn't really very much else to do in Whitchurch village of an evening.

When we arrived outside the Ponty's bright yellow walls, the first thing we noticed was the absence of a queue. Gareth stopped short in the street and said, 'Crikey! I'd have thought *Love, Lies and Secrets* would be more of a crowd-puller. *The*

Western Mail described it as the romance of the year. The bloke who does the reviews said it's guaranteed to put ladies in the loving mood.' And then Gareth coughed and added, 'Of course, it ain't my kind of film but I thought you might like it.'

I looked in at the deserted foyer and said, 'Maybe we're late.'

Gareth looked worried and pushed open the door. Inside, had it not been for some carol-singing coal-miners who were blaring too loudly out of a single tinny speaker set high up on the wall, it would have been just as quiet as it looked from outside. Pat Mumble was reading a copy of *Celebrity Dirt* magazine and looking bored. Next to her, my best friend Goose, dressed in the most atrocious electric blue and yellow uniform I'd ever seen, was playing with her mobile phone and looking even more bored. When she saw us, her face brightened.

'Lottie!' she said, loud enough to be heard above a choral Welsh version of *Silent Night*.

'Goosey! I said, loud enough to be heard back. And then I gestured towards the solitary speaker and said, 'What the heck is this horrible music?'

'The Fron Male Voice Choir,' replied Goose. 'Helluva festive. It really puts you in the Christmas mood.' And then she pointed at me with both index fingers, wiggled her head on her neck and said, 'Lady Lottie Lala has entered the building!' After that, she said, 'Hi, Gareth.'

Gareth said, 'Hi, Goose,' and I wiggled my head back at her and said, 'Missy Goosey Gaga is in the house!'

Goose said, 'Lady Lottie Hottie—'

Pat Mumble coughed.

Goose sat up straighter, put on her sensible face and said, 'Can I help you?'

'Yeah, can we have two tickets for *Love, Lies and Secrets*?' said Gareth, who seemed a bit embarrassed for some reason.

Pat Mumble crunched on a sweet and said, 'Mumble mumble mumble Love, Lies and Secrets mumble mumble mumble screaming.'

Me and Gareth both said, 'Wah?'

Goose, who had been watching with a look of pained concentration on her face as Pat Mumble spoke, lowered her voice and asked, 'Mumble mumble mumble finished mumble mumble?'

Pat Mumble mumbled something back.

Goose nodded and turned back to us. '*Love, Lies and Secrets* finished this afternoon. The only film we're showing tonight is *And They Died Screaming*.'

Gareth's face fell. 'I don't fancy the sound of that.' Looking around the empty foyer, he added, 'Don't seem like anyone else does either.'

Pat Mumble said, 'Kids mumble mumble mumble clear off then mumble.'

After a slight delay and more pained concentration, Goose turned red, mumbled something back to Pat Mumble and then said to us, 'Did you want to see the film or not? It starts in a few minutes.'

'What's it about?' asked Gareth.

'Er . . . perhaps I can assist?' A nervous voice behind us caused us to spin round. Dressed in the kind of jumper that should have a Government Nerd Warning stamped on it,

Tim, the geeky sixth-former, was hovering awkwardly, half in and half out of a doorway marked *Staff Only*. I couldn't help noticing that, instead of the putrid blue and yellow uniform, he was wearing jeans with pleats in them and a hand-knitted jumper that had a pattern of film directors' clapperboards all over it. In this context, Goose's uniform suddenly seemed fairly reasonable. Tim *was* wearing the regulation Ponty-Carlo staff badge though. As he was standing so close, I took the opportunity to read what was on it:

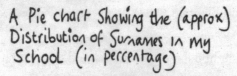

**Ponty-Carlo Picture House
Staff
Tim Overup**

My initial thought was that you don't tend to meet many people with the surname Overup in Wales. In fact, in my school, I'd say that the distribution of surnames is probably something very close to this:

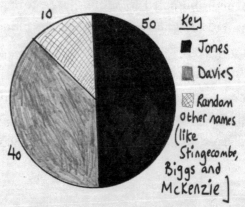

A Pie chart Showing the (approx) Distribution of Surnames in my School (in percentage)

Key
■ Jones
▨ Davies
▧ Random other names (like Stingecombe, Biggs and McKenzie)

10
50
40

I've definitely never encountered an Overup before.

My second thought was something far more wondrous. I'm a person who has always had a fascination with backward names. As it happens, my own backward name is very boring and, when said aloud, quite displeasing to the ear. Sggib Eitoll. Or Sggib Ettolrahc to people who aren't close personal friends. Some people, however, have very interesting backward names. It took me about four seconds to work out that Tim Overup is definitely one of them. In fact, Tim Overup has the funniest and most fantastically brilliant backward name I've ever come across in my entire life! And I don't say that lightly because one of Goose's former lovers was Neil Adam the Mad Alien. But Tim's name is even better! I almost howled out loud on the spot. Thankfully, I didn't though. I have got *some* manners.

Tim Overup pushed a stray piece of gingery hair away from his eyes and, flashing a nervous grin, said, 'I . . . um . . . heard your deliberations as to whether or not you should see tonight's feature. Well . . . um . . . having *myself* been the individual solely responsible for arranging the screening of this . . . er . . . film, I might be able to . . . er . . . help you make up your mind.'

'Oh,' said Gareth. 'Cheers, mate. What's it about?'

Tim rubbed his elbow and frowned thoughtfully. 'I . . . um . . . suppose one is obliged to categorize it as horror but this does seem to . . . er . . . rather underplay the art house influences of its production.' He paused for a moment to blow his nose on a gigantic handkerchief, which he'd pulled out of a pocket in his jeans. Then, after carefully tucking the hanky away again, he added, 'Its director, Attila Nagy, is very much at the forefront of . . . um . . . European new wave cinema. You'll find as you watch it . . . if indeed you *choose* to watch it . . . that he likes to use the camera just as a writer would use a pen and . . . um . . . this allows the film to sort of write itself . . . organically . . . if you know what I mean?'

I didn't. Judging by the look of confusion on Gareth's face, I don't think Gareth did either. I looked at Pat Mumble. She was crunching sweets on her wooden teeth and reading *Celebrity Dirt* magazine again. Only Goose looked like she had any clue what Tim was on about. To my surprise, she was nodding enthusiastically.

Tim continued. 'The overall effect is one of a terrifyingly deranged stream of consciousness.'

Goose was nodding so hard in agreement that I thought her head might fall off. I narrowed my eyes suspiciously, and addressing her directly, I said, 'Stream of what?'

'Stream of *consciousness*,' said Goose, without a second's hesitation. 'It's an uninterrupted artistic outpouring designed to convey the raw experience of the artist or artistic creation.'

'Oh,' I said. And then I shut my mouth.

Gareth said, 'Is it scary though?'

Gareth doesn't like scary films. The last time we saw a horror film together, he had to leave the cinema early so that he could be sick. To be fair though, this probably had less to do with the film and more to do with the fact that he'd eaten a gigantic bucket of toffee popcorn, a bag of chocolate peanuts and a choc ice before the film had even started. And then I'd completely pushed him over the edge by trying to touch his nudger while we were in the dark. I WON'T EVER DO THAT AGAIN.

Tim put his head on one side. 'Is it scary? Um . . . yes, yes. But it's . . . um . . . intelligent psychological terror rather than . . . um . . . mindless wanton violence. And it's only a certificate twelve but . . . of course, if you have an . . . um . . . nervous disposition then . . .'

'OK. Thanks, mate,' said Gareth hurriedly, and then turning back to Goose, he said, 'We'll have two tickets for this screaming thing then, please.' And then to Pat Mumble he said, 'And two regular colas, a regular toffee popcorn and a bar of out-of-date chocolate.' Slapping his stomach he grinned and added, 'Don't wanna be overdoing it, do I?'

Goose thumped a rubber stamp into an inkpad and then stamped the backs of our hands with the Ponty-Carlo logo. It looks like this.

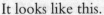

I can see now where Tim Overup got the inspiration for his dodgy jumper.

Despite the fact that everyone always asks for a ticket, nobody actually gets given one unless they've booked ahead. Goose reckons that this is because the Ponty-Carlo is more environmentally friendly than most other cinemas and is doing its bit to use up less of the world's paper. This argument would hold up fine if it wasn't for the fact that it's actually using up ridiculous and unnecessary quantities of the world's soap. The Ponty-Carlo's rubber stamp refuses to shift from the skin until at least five days have passed and half a tonne of soap has been used in the attempt to remove it. Whenever my mum sees this stamp on my hand, she likes to go through this hilarious rigmarole of pretending she doesn't know what it is. She says, 'It can't stand for Police Constable because you aren't one . . . and it can't stand for Personal Computer because you aren't one of those either. I *don't think* it means Politically Correct because you aren't particularly . . . so it must mean *Please Clean*.' If there was a law against making boring jokes, my mum would be locked up for life.

As she took our money, Goose said in a low voice, 'I've got to help Tim in the projection room for a bit but sit near the back and I'll come and join you later on. It's totally dead in here tonight anyway.'

Pushing open the door to the screen room, it immediately became apparent that Goose was right. It *was* dead. As Gareth and I headed towards the back, I counted only seven seats that were occupied. To my horror, I noticed that one of these seven occupants was wearing a pair of cyber-goggles around her neck.

'I don't chuffing believe it!' I said, nudging Gareth harder than I'd actually meant to and causing him to spill a few toffee popcorns over the blue and gold carpet. 'STEVIE WONDER'S DAUGHTER IS HERE!'

'WHAT? WHERE?' Gareth abruptly halted and looked wildly around him. 'Isn't Stevie Wonder massively famous? What would his daughter be doing at the Ponty-Carlo?'

'Not *that* Stevie Wonder,' I said. 'I mean the Stevie Wonder who's going out with my mum.'

For some reason, Gareth couldn't have heard me properly. His eyes widened in shock and, lowering his voice to a hushed whisper, he said, 'Your ... mum ... is GOING OUT with STEVIE WONDER? I thought you said she was seeing some boring old police bloke? Oh my God, Lottie, that's immense!' And then he started waving his elbows about and humming the tune to 'Thriller' – even though it was blatantly a song by Michael Jackson. More of our popcorn tumbled to the floor.

I stood in the aisle of the cinema and gave Gareth a hard look. It wasn't exactly a Stare of Death but it was dangerously close.

'WHAT?' said Gareth, raising his box of popcorn up to head height so that he could tip a few in the direction of his mouth. 'What have I said?'

And then a funny thing happened. Life stepped in and

stopped me making a total turnip of myself. Thank God it did! Because I was just on the very brink of a severely stroppy outburst which could have ruined my relationship with Gareth forever. But then the lights dimmed and the curtains that covered the screen jerked backwards. There, in big massive letters, I read the words:

'Genius is Eternal Patience'

A Short Film about the Life of Michelangelo

Now, I've learned a thing or two about Michelangelo during my art lessons. I happen to know that he painted the ceiling of the Sistine Chapel in Rome and I know that he was also the man who gave the world this:

This is a statue of someone called David. For the sake of modern decency, I have made one very slight but extremely necessary adjustment to Michelangelo's original masterpiece. Personally, I think David would be relieved. But, naked statues aside, Michelangelo was still an exceptionally clever man. He was a painter, a sculptor, an architect and an engineer. Judging from the title of this film, I'd guess that like me he was also a bit of a philosopher. And even though I'm no genius, it doesn't take a whole heap of intelligence to work out that Michelangelo considered patience to be a very admirable thing. And suddenly, despite the fact that I was being stalked by an emo in cyber-goggles, and despite even that my mum was probably at that very same second feeding grapes[13] to Detective Sergeant Giles of the South Wales Police, I felt a serious and mysterious and delirious rush of intense happiness. Because, right there and then, none of that actually mattered. But what really *did* matter was the fact that my lovely gorgeous boyfriend wanted to spend his entire Saturday evening with me. Even though I'm an uptight biscuit-brain with high levels of woman tension. And if that doesn't make Gareth David Lloyd George Stingecombe a totally terrific genius than I really don't know what does.

---

[13] Or whatever other pukesome disgusting thing it is that middle-aged people do when they're being flirty with each other.

aND theY DIeD sCreamING

The entertainment at the Ponty went downhill from there. Because as soon as the title for the main feature appeared on the screen, I just knew that it wasn't going to be my cup of tea. Or coffee. Or anything. In fact, I had exactly the same sort of crappy cheated feeling that I get when I jump into a big full-to-the-brim bubble bath and find out that the water isn't quite hot enough or when my PE teacher tells us we're going for a nice long cross-country run in the rain. In front of me were the words . . .

És Sikítottak Mikőzben Meghaltak

(And They Died Screaming)

'What language is that?' I whispered to Gareth.

Gareth frowned. Then, after a moment or two, he whispered back, 'It definitely ain't Welsh. Or French. Could well be Russian though. Or Irish.' He crammed a handful of popcorn into his mouth and chewed thoughtfully.

Then he said, 'Mind you, there's a good possibility that it's Portuguese.' After another pause, he added, 'Or Dutch.' Picking up his cola, he sucked on the straw, his forehead still creased in concentration. Then, with a confident nod, he concluded, 'Having said that, it's probably Polish.' After that, he put his arm around me and said, 'But to be strictly honest with you, Lotts, I ain't totally sure.'

This is one of the things I absolutely love about Gareth. He always puts his heart and soul into everything he does. Even when what he's trying to do is physically impossible or completely out of his knowledge zone, he will always try to find an answer. If he hadn't decided to devote his life to the game of rugby, I think he could have made a pretty good philosopher.

I was still a bit bothered about the stuff written on the screen though so instead of telling him this, I whispered, 'Oh brilliant. It's gonna be one of those weird films where you have to *read* the subtitles just to give yourself the faintest clue what's happening. I hate reading!'

Gareth laughed and poked me in the stomach. 'No you don't! You're always reading!'

'Oh jog on!' I said. 'I don't mind reading books but that's about as far as I'm prepared to take it.' And then I poked Gareth back.

The film started. On the screen, a little girl with her hair plaited into two long pigtails was whizzing backwards and forwards on a swing in an empty playground that was surrounded by derelict concrete tower blocks. The whole thing was shot in black and white. I let out a noisy sigh and, poking Gareth again, I whispered, 'I hate black and white films. They bore my brains out!'

Gareth removed his arm from across my shoulders and, taking hold of my hand, laced his fingers through mine. 'Seriously, babe . . .' he whispered, '. . . are you gonna moan all the way through this? Cos I ain't being funny, Lotts, but you're starting to make my ears bleed.'

In the early days of our relationship, Gareth was extremely sweet and seemed totally blown away by my very existence. I could have happily moaned through fifteen films in a row and he wouldn't have uttered a single word of disapproval. I've been going out with him for a while now and I've noticed that the dynamic between us has shifted a bit. He's still very sweet but nowadays he tends to tell me when I'm doing his head in. If anything, I think this makes him even more desirable.

I stuck my tongue out at him in the darkness and turned my attention back to the screen. The girl was still swinging. There was no sound at all except for that of the swing which was really, really creaky. Nothing else was happening. It was just this little girl swinging backwards and forwards all on her own in the middle of an empty playground in the middle of empty tower blocks. Backwards and forwards. Backwards and forwards. It went on and on and on. The only noise in the whole cinema was this:

Squeak
Creak
Squeak
Creak
Squeak
Creak

It was squeakily creakily freaky. I looked at my watch. Six minutes had passed and that little girl was still swinging.

I nudged Gareth. 'Do you think the film has got stuck?'

Gareth frowned. 'I dunno. She's been on that swing a while, hasn't she? It's a wonder she ain't totally dizzy. Perhaps that Tim bloke has nodded off in the projection room.' And then he waved a piece of popcorn happily at the screen and said, 'Oh no . . . look . . . something else is happening.'

Eager not to miss any dramatic development in the storyline, we both leaned forward in our seats but then slumped back again with bitter disappointment when we realized that the only thing that had changed was the camera angle. The little girl was *still* swinging but now we were viewing the scene from behind. Not for the first time,

I let out a noisy sigh. 'Where do you think Goose is?' I whispered. 'She said she was going to come and sit with us.'

Gareth nudged me and nodded towards the door. 'I reckon this must be her now.'

Coming towards us through the darkness was the pale beam of a cheap torch and the occasional flash of an electric blue and yellow uniform. I lifted my feet so that my trainers were resting snugly on the back of the seat in front of me and waved the torch over.

The little girl continued to swing.

The torchlight halted by my chair. I squinted into it and said, 'Goose?'

A voice – which was blatantly not Goose's – said, 'Mumble mumble . . . feet down . . . mumble mumble.'

Almost jumping out of my skin, I whipped my feet off the chair in front and sat bolt upright in my seat. Even though the cinema was practically empty and she could have sat anywhere, Pat Mumble plonked herself down directly behind me. For the billionth time I sighed. Gareth squeezed my hand and failed to suppress a chuckle. The little girl continued to swing. And then, in that weird language which definitely wasn't Welsh or French but might have been Russian, Irish, Portuguese, Dutch or Polish, she began to chant. It sounded like a nursery rhyme and, as she swung, she chanted the same words over and over again. Subtitles came up on the screen to help us. Painfully aware of Pat Mumble's presence in my very close rear proximity, I frowned at the screen and read . . .

The candle is burning, burning,

Don't let it out,

Those who want to see the flame

Should all crouch down.

I shivered. Pat Mumble leaned forward so that I could smell her furniture-polish breath and said, 'Mumble mumble . . . gets worse . . . mumble.' And then I heard her rip the paper off a Cornetto.

Abruptly, the scene changed and cut to an image of chimpanzees in a jungle. There were loads of them sitting in the treetops and they were all making a truly horrible high-pitched shrieking sound. Some of the chimps were furiously beating their chests and all of them had their mouths wide open revealing massively sharp teeth. Usually, I'm extremely interested in film footage of monkeys and other swinging primates. I'm especially interested in orang-utans who – along with rabbits and chinchillas – are my most favourite animals on the planet. I didn't like this clip of film though. Not one bit. To be honest, it was putting me really massively totally on edge.

Behind me, Pat Mumble was noisily sucking on her ice cream. To my left, Gareth's body was shaking and I knew he was having another fit of the silent chuckles. Putting his mouth close to my ear, he whispered, 'This film is nuts! I'm loving it!' And then he clamped his hand over his mouth to stop himself from chuckling his head off.

I wasn't chuckling though. 'I don't like it,' I whispered.

Instantly, Gareth's mood changed and his face turned serious. 'It's OK, babe,' he whispered back to me. 'I'll protect you.' And then he kissed me on the forehead and wrapped his arm around me. I put my fingers in my ears and snuggled up next to his body.

The shrieking chimpanzees faded away. Before I could breathe a sigh of relief, however, the film cut back to the swing. It was still going backwards and forwards exactly as it had done before – except that this time there was no girl sitting on it. She had disappeared. The swing was now moving all by itself. Backwards and forwards. Backwards and forwards. Backwards and forwards. On and on and on. Behind me Pat Mumble was demolishing her ice cream like it was the last ice cream she was ever going to eat. Even though my fingers were still in my ears, I obviously wasn't pressing hard enough because all I could hear was:

Squeak
Creak
Slurp
Squeak
Creak
Slurp

. . . over and over again.

I started to feel a bit ill.

The swing vanished and was replaced by the image of a fat butcher with a bushy grey moustache wearing a blood-stained apron. My heart sank. The butcher was wrapping bits of meat – they might have been pork chops – in sheets of greaseproof paper. Sometimes, before he wrapped a chop, he'd give it a little squeeze, making a few drops of blood drip on to his meat-splattered work surface. My heart sank a little lower. Gareth's right hand stroked my right shoulder. Pat Mumble, evidently having finished all the ice cream, began to crunch on her wafer cone. My heart continued to sink and, little by little, I felt my stomach start to rise. Gareth's hand stopped stroking my shoulder and began to drift downward.

I still wasn't feeling too good.

The butcher slapped a juicy pork chop on to a pair of weighing scales. Pat Mumble let out a contented burp and said, 'Mumble mumble pardon.' I shifted uncomfortably in my seat.

I really didn't feel good.

And then three things which should never ever have been connected in my mind – but which now, tragically, always will be – occurred at the exact same moment.

1. Pat Mumble squeezed out another burp.
2. The butcher squeezed a pork chop.
3. Gareth's right hand squeezed my right boob.

In a total panic, I stood up. 'I'm sorry, Gaz,' I said. 'I feel totally hanging!'[14] And then I rushed out through the back door fire exit.

The cinema foyer was still completely quiet. The shutters were down in front of the tills and nobody was about. I walked over to the kiosk where Pat Mumble stands our cups of not-Coke-and-not-Pepsi-cola and folded my arms on the counter. Then I lowered my head into my arms and stood there, slumped against the refreshments counter, and concentrated really hard on containing my inner vomit.

Behind me a door creaked open. A vision of the swinging girl flashed into my mind and made me groan. A voice said, 'Lottie? What are you doing out here? Are you OK?'

It was Goose's voice.

Without lifting my head, I twisted my face to look at her and said, 'It all got a bit intense in there and I nearly puked!' And then I said, 'Where did you get to? I thought you were coming in to join us?'

Goose's face flushed. 'Oh yeah . . . sorry . . . I was helping Tim in the projection room.'

'Well, you didn't miss much,' I grumbled. 'Just a swinger, some pork and a bit of monkey business.' And then, even though I still felt terrible, I chuckled because I'd effortlessly made that stupid film sound a million times more interesting than it actually was. I should get a job in advertising or something.

Goose came and joined me by the refreshments counter

---

[14] Hanging means the same as minging. Not to be confused with banging, which means stonking.

and sympathetically stroked the back of my head. 'You poor thing,' she said. 'You look helluva green. Do you want a drink or something? I could get you a Coke . . . well . . . I mean more of a cola-flavoured carbonated soft drink?'

'Yuck, no thanks,' I replied. 'My stomach is heaving as it is. That film totally messed me up.'

Goose nodded and continued to stroke my hair. 'I haven't had a chance to see it yet but Tim really rates it. He reckons that it makes more sense if you consider it as a piece of conceptual art rather than purely seeing it as an entertainment form. Tim is writing about it for his Film Studies A level. Tim reckons that—'

But I never got to hear what else Tim Overup reckoned. The door leading from Screen One swung open and we were interrupted by two more people fleeing the film. Too late, I noticed that one of them was wearing a pair of cyber-goggles around her neck. The other one was a skinny boy with long skinny hair and skinny dark trousers and the chunkiest pair of devil boots on his feet that I'd ever seen in my whole life. His legs and feet combination looked like this.

Those boots still didn't make him taller than his lanky girlfriend though.

'All right?' said Lois to me.

'All right?' I said to Lois.

Lois sniffed and gave me a brief nod. Jerking her head back towards the screen door, she asked, 'You couldn't hack the film then?'

I shrugged. And then, realizing I still had my head crashed out on the counter, I smiled a bit and admitted, 'Not much. Couldn't you?'

Lois gawped at me like I was a freakoid in a cage. 'We've seen heaps of films heaps more messed up than that! That one was too soft for us.' Then she dipped her hand down the front of her top, rummaged around for a moment and magically pulled a mobile phone out from between her twin-peak personal regions. Raising it in front of her, she said, 'I've sooooo got to put a picture of you up on Facebook. You look completely siiiiick!'

I stood up really quickly then and stretched my arm out in front of me in order to block her lens with my palm. 'Er . . . no thanks,' I said. 'Call me weird if you like but I don't actually like unflattering photos of myself being plastered all over the internet for any old freak to look at.'

Lois put her phone back down her bra. 'Suit yourself. Loads of people would've poked you though.'

I was worried then that I'd come across as a bit uptight so I said, 'I'll add you as a friend if you like.' This was a lie. There's no way she will ever be my friend. Even in cyberspace.

Lois said, 'Lucky lucky me.' And then she and the little big-boot man started laughing all their spurs and studs off. Not with me. But blatantly at me. And just when I thought the conversation couldn't get any more awful, Lois rummaged around in her bra again, produced a watch which was attached to a chain, looked at it and said, 'Do you reckon my dad is still at your mum's?'

I said, 'How the heck should I know?'

Goose said, 'What?'

I said, 'I'll tell you about it later.'

Lois laughed at me again and said, 'Your mum fancies my dad. Deal with it!'

And I said, 'Deal with your hair, why don't you. Your roots are showing.'

Lois glared at me over her eyeliner. Then she dropped her watch back down her purple leopard-print top, pulled her cyber-goggles up into position and said to the little big-boot man, 'Come on Morys, let's ditch this dive.' And with that, Lois and Morys left the building.

When they'd gone, Goose shook her head. 'That was one helluva bad attitude! Who the heck was *she*?' And then she added, 'And what was all that stuff about your mum and her dad?'

I opened my mouth to explain but no words came out. Instead, I just stood there staring silently at Goose like I was some kind of stupid five-foot (and a fraction over half an inch) tall goldfish. I didn't know how to even begin to answer Goose's question. More to the point, I didn't want to. Thankfully, before I had a chance to try, Gareth came crashing through the doors. He was holding my coat and the last of the popcorn. When he spotted me, his face lit up with relief. 'Oh there you are!' Then he paused and looked a bit embarrassed. 'Sorry I didn't come out straight away . . . I thought perhaps you might need a bit of space and . . . anyway, there was this really interesting bit where the film cut back to the swing and it had been all tied up in a knot and was just hanging there motionless and I wanted to see if anything weird was gonna happen but then it cut back to the screaming monkeys so I came out to look for you.' And then he turned to Goose and said, 'Is she OK?'

Goose said, 'Yeah. The film made her feel a bit weird though.'

Gareth looked a bit worried and said, 'Oh.' He glanced at me anxiously and then, turning back to Goose again, he said, 'Do you think she'll be OK to walk home?'

Goose said, 'I reckon so. You might have to carry her though.'

Gareth looked even more worried and said, 'Oh. Do you think she—'

'Excuse me,' I said. 'I *am* still here, you know!'

Gareth said, 'Oh, right, yeah. Sorry, Lottie.' And then he said to Goose, 'Do you want us to hang around and walk home with you?'

'No no no,' said Goose. 'It's OK. Tim has just passed his driving test – he'll give me a lift. Or Pat will.'

Something about the way she said this made me raise my eyebrows but I don't think either of them noticed because my head was still flat out on the refreshments counter. To be honest, I was rather shocked by the idea that Goose preferred to be accompanied home by either Pat Mumble or Pure Vomit rather than by me and Gareth – but I was still feeling too spaced out to bother saying anything.

'Suit yourself,' said Gareth and then he helped me into my coat and said, 'Come on, Biggsy, let's get you out of here.'

Alone, on the pavement outside, we paused for a moment under the shelter of the cinema's canopy and looked at the snow, which was now coming down quite hard. Gareth took my hand and coughed. 'Look, Lottie,' he began awkwardly, 'I'm totally sorry I touched your jubbly. No offence like.'

'None taken,' I said.

Gareth looked relieved and smiled at me in the snow. 'Tonight turned out to be fairly rubbish, didn't it? Shall we pretend it never happened?'

'Yeah,' I said. 'You can erase everything about this evening from your mind – except for this bit.' And then I stood on my tiptoes and kissed him. Really passionately. For fifty-two seconds.

When we finally stopped, Gareth gripped hold of my hand and said, 'Wow!' His eyes lingered on mine and – not for the first time – I was helplessly captivated in a highly romantic eye-lock. Without really knowing why, I held my breath. In a weirdly wobbly voice, Gareth said, 'I love YouTube.'

And then he coughed and started frowning down at his K-Swiss trainers which were getting all wet and slushy in the snow, and the romantic spell was not exactly broken but definitely weakened a little bit.

'What?' I said.

'YouTube,' said Gareth, coughing again and clearing his throat. 'The online location to discover, watch, upload and share videos. I love the fact that it allows me to watch victorious moments from the golden age of Welsh rugby and weekly highlights of the Cardiff Blues in the comfort of my own bedroom.'

'Oh,' I said, slightly confused. 'Thanks for sharing that fact with me.'

'No worries,' said Gareth, and then he gave me a heart-stoppingly sweet smile and dragged me out into the snow. 'Come on, Biggsy, I'll walk you home.'

And he did. And we kissed again on my doorstep – for seventy-six seconds – and I stood and watched him with a warm jittery wriggle in my stomach as he went skidding and sliding off down the street in the direction of his own house. He looked ever so heroic. A bit like a young Scott of the Antarctic.

But without the hat, skis or coat.

But that's enough about Gareth for now. And enough about everything. It's time to hit the Save button, shut down this computer and climb into my lovely snuggly bed. It's ten past midnight and if my mum realizes how long I've spent sitting in front of this computer, she'll have a total screaming hissy fit and ban me from using it ever again. And that's not a risk I'm prepared to take. Because I'm sick of arguing with her. And I wouldn't be at all surprised if she's sick of arguing with me too.

a Brief wOrD aBOut the tOtaLLY raNDOm Nature Of sChOOL assemBLY

I am about to write something very unusual. It's certainly not anything I've ever written before. In fact, the sentence I am about to type is so massively, incredibly, unbelievably improbable, that I wouldn't be at all surprised if it has never previously been put down on paper by anyone ever. Here goes:

Assembly was really interesting today.

Honestly, it was.

In fact, it provided the only interesting moment in an otherwise amazingly boring week. Monday and Tuesday, I had tests in maths, science and history; Wednesday, a careers talk replaced my art lesson; Thursday, Mr Wood tried to teach us all how to use apostrophes again; and today, I just couldn't be arsed to listen any more. Except in assembly. Because, as I just said, it was surprisingly interesting.

Now don't get me wrong; I never intended to approach the subject of assembly with a negative attitude. I think, *in theory*, that the concept of a shared intellectual moment first thing on a Friday morning is a really sensible one. After all, in weeks like the one I've just had, it can provide the only chance of an intellectual moment we're actually going to get. Especially if the supply teachers are in. *In practice*, however, there are two serious issues that need some major attention.

1. We have to sit on the floor and it's really uncomfortable and makes our clothes dusty.
2. 99.9% of our assemblies are a pile of random horse plop.

These are not opinions. They are facts. I'd even go as far as to say that they are unsatisfactory facts. Take, as evidence, the assembly we had last week. Mr Wood was in the spotlight. I like Mr Wood because he's my English teacher and English is one of my all-time favourite subjects – but that doesn't alter the undeniable truth that Mr Wood has an unfortunate tendency to be spectacularly dull. Picture the scene. We're all sitting there, cramped together on the floor, and Mr Wood walks on to the stage and says, 'Good morning, Year Eleven.'

And we all say, 'Grumble mumble, Mr Wood.'

And then Mr Wood opens his mouth and says, 'The other month, my wife went into a well-known large electrical retailer in the centre of Cardiff to purchase a vacuum cleaner *blah blah blah-di-blah* . . .'

And he goes on and on and on – and my bottom is aching because it's not as fashionably fat as Beyoncé's or J-Lo's, and Gareth has started fiddling slyly with his iPod, and Beca Bowen has got her tweezers out and is sneakily plucking her eyebrows, and still Mr Wood is just standing there in the middle of the stage, droning on to nobody and saying things like, '*blah blah* . . . the Dyson dual cyclone bagless vacuum cleaner *blah blah* . . .'

And while he drones on, I'm aware of Gareth's sweet feet tapping in time to the music which is now blaring noiselessly through the single earphone hidden behind his upturned collar and I'm aware too of Beca Bowen flicking her putrid eyebrow hairs all over the place and I'm seriously worried that my head might explode and my backside might implode because I'm so downright bored and uncomfortable.

And then, just when I think I'm about to die of Drone's Disease, Mr Wood says something along the lines of, 'So, Year Eleven, that brings me to the message of today's assembly. *If*, like James Dyson, you are unable to find a vacuum cleaner which fulfils all your cleaning requirements to a satisfactory standard, you should do something about it and *invent your own*.' And then he shuffles off the stage and we're finally allowed to get up off our numb bums and shuffle off to our first lesson.

Random or what?

And then there's the assembly which Mrs Leigh-Lewis gave the week before. That was worse. Mrs Leigh-Lewis is our head teacher and we don't see her very often because she hardly ever comes out of her office. To be honest, I don't think she's too comfortable with the harsh – but honest – lighting of our school corridors. The boys in our school call her The Soft Focus Fox. Her hair is styled into an immaculate blonde bob, her face is coated in a thick layer of make-up and her nails are shaped into really long sharp points, which are painted red. Seen in dim light, fuzzy vision or from a reasonable distance, she looks stunningly glamorous. If you get a proper look at her though, she's dead wrinkly. The teachers like to refer to her as Gerry. For some reason which totally escapes me, they all think that this is hilariously witty and funny.[15] I have no idea why Gerry Leigh-Lewis embarked upon a teaching career because she absolutely hates the lot of us. She does love her *own* children though. And she loves herself. We know this because she is always telling us. The last assembly we had with her went something like this:

Mrs L-L: Good morning, Year Eleven.

Us: Mumble grumble, Mrs Leigh-Lewis.

Mrs L-L: Today's assembly is about respect. Respect. One little word. One gigantic concept. So often, as I go about my daily business, I hear pupils demanding that they be treated with respect and yet we cannot demand respect, we have to earn it. I, of course, have earned it because I've got a first class honours degree from Salford University and a Master's degree with a distinction from Cardiff – not to mention years and years of a fantastic teaching career under my belt, so I do expect respect. And I've earned the right to expect it. As have

<hr>

[15] Her first name is Geraldine. So what?

all of the teachers in this assembly hall. But you haven't automatically earned that right. You need to start earning it right here and right now in this school. And then maybe, one day, you too will be a focus for the admiration and respect of others.

Mrs Leigh-Lewis pauses meaningfully. Gareth fiddles secretly with his iPod, Beca Bowen shiftily puts some lipstick on and my bum aches. Mrs Leigh-Lewis folds her arms, glares down on us and says:

Let me tell you a story.

Gareth taps his feet happily, Beca Bowen moves on to her eyebrows, and approximately two hundred other people (me included) give a silent inner sigh of despair and misery.

Last weekend, my daughter went to a party. Have I told you about my daughter? No? Well, her name is Rosie and she is beautiful. She is also extremely clever. Anyway, last weekend, Rosie went to a party. It was a fancy dress party. And the theme of that fancy dress party was to go dressed up as someone you admire. Someone you respect. And do you know who Rosie chose to go as? Do you? No, of course you don't. Well, let me tell you. Rosie, my beautiful and clever daughter, went to that fancy dress party dressed as me. Because *I* am someone she respects and admires. Thank you, Year Eleven. Have a good day.

Like I said before. Roger Random.

But this morning's assembly was different. In fact, it was a breath of fresh air. Because I actually got something out of it. I had a meaningful moment! And I have Mr Davies to thank for that. He's an RE man by trade.

Mr Davies walked on to the stage carrying a large tray of eggs. He carefully placed the tray down on the ground, put his head thoughtfully on one side and said, *'Hmmm?'* And then he said, 'Good morning, Year Eleven.'

And we all said, 'Mumble grumble, Mr Davies.'

And Mr Davies gave one quick little intake of breath, organized his right hand so that it looked as if he was aiming an air dart at us and said, 'I'm an RE man by trade. Religion in all its many rainbow-coloured aspects is my daily bread and butter. It pays the bills. It puts food on the table. It keeps the wolf from the door. *Hmmm?* So when Mrs Leigh-Lewis asked me to lead the assembly today, I jumped at the opportunity and asked myself which parable I should share with you young people. Which religious lesson? *Hmmm?'*

Cramped up, cross-legged on the floor, I felt my brain closing down. I'm a hard-headed, practical woman of philosophy by trade. I don't do religion. Further down the row, I spotted Gareth turning his collar up. Beca Bowen pulled a compact mirror out of one of her Knuggs.[16] On the stage, Mr Davies continued to aim his imaginary dart at us.

Taking another sharp intake of breath, he made a sort of

---

[16] Knitted Ugg boots. Obviously.

quick chewing motion which was accompanied by the noise '*schlop schlop*' and then launched back into his speech.

'But then I decided against all that. Cardiff is a wonderfully diverse city. And this school is a wonderfully diverse place. *Hmmm?* And I don't want to alienate anyone by talking of *this* belief or *that* belief so I thought I'd stick to something we can *all* believe in. Tolerance. That's right. Tolerance. *Hmmm? Hmmm?*'

Gareth's elbows were resting on his knees and his head was resting in his palms. I could see his fingers tapping against his ears in time to whatever bass line he was listening to. Beca Bowen was gluing on false eyelashes. My own eyes were starting to close. Mr Davies chewed briskly on his saliva . . .

. . . *schlop*

schlop

. . . bent down, picked up one of his eggs and smashed it on the stage. Gareth pulled his earphone out. Beca Bowen poked herself in the eye. My own eyelids flew back open and I sat up straighter.

Mr Davies looked down at the broken egg and said, 'That egg, Year Eleven, represents intolerance. It represents what happens when we cannot accept each other. When we cannot co-exist happily. People get hurt. Things get broken. But it doesn't have to be like that. Tolerance and understanding make us all stronger. When we all stand together, we are invincible.'

Mr Davies pulled another egg out of his pocket, stooped down and placed it in the empty slot in his egg tray. Then he stopped aiming his imaginary dart at us and aimed it at the eggs.

'This tray of eggs represents us. Some of us are white. Some of us are brown. We are big, small, speckled . . . some of us are a bit grubby even. *Hmmm?* And individually, we are quite fragile. Quite vulnerable. Like that broken egg – *SCHLOP SCHLOP* – But if we can just learn to accept each other – tolerate each other – and live together, side by side, we will all be so much the stronger for it. Let me show you something.'

From the wings of the stage, two burly sixth-form boys appeared. Mr Davies placed a flat square of wood over his tray of eggs. The sixth-formers grasped hold of Mr Davies from either side and hoisted him very very gently on to the tray of eggs. And then they stood back and left him balanced there, perilously.

Mr Davies is not a thin man.

The whole of Year 11 looked at this bizarre scene in total and utter amazement and then, because we were all quite shocked, we started clapping and wolf-whistling.

The sixth-formers lifted Mr Davies back on to solid

ground and then one of them removed the piece of wood to reveal that all the eggs were still intact. Mr Davies waited, centre stage, for us to quieten down again. Finally, when we had, he said, 'Three words to take away with you today. Tolerance. Understanding. Strength. *Hmmm?* Thank you, Year Eleven.'

And then he cleared up his broken egg and left the hall.

And I've been thinking about Davo and his eggs all day. And I've been thinking about those words too. And even though the idea of my mum and Stevie Wonder being an item makes me want to hit things with a hammer, I'm going to try to tolerate him and understand where my mum is coming from. And hopefully, that will make me a much stronger and nicer person.

keePING MY eGGs INtaCt

I've survived the first test. Stevie Wonder came round our house for his lunch today, and me and him politely shared our first proper social engagement. Despite a few early hiccups, I think I handled it all fairly well. Especially when you consider the latest difficult development in my life: I am afflicted with GREY hair!

Stevie is quickly becoming a regular fixture in my mum's life. In fact, I'd go as far as to say that they are already practically inseparable. Last Saturday night, he was still sitting on the sofa when I got back from the cinema and I didn't hear him leave until . . .

Then, yesterday, he took my mum out for a drink after they'd both finished work and earlier today he was sniffing around again wanting to be fed. And this is, of course, in addition to the fact that they see each other every single day of the week because they work in the same police station.

My mum must be nutty noodles about him.

She even laid the table with napkins and place mats although at the weekends we normally just eat our meals from plastic trays on our laps while we sit in the living room and watch programmes with titles like *Fat Britain: Out of Control*. But this morning, my mum was up at dawn's crack, and I could hear the vacuum cleaner roaring and the washing machine spinning and I knew she was up to something. Because, when she's not out chasing criminals, Saturday morning is usually reserved for a big lie-in. Even though my mum has single-handedly reduced crime in Cardiff by approximately four-fifths, there are still faint traces of a naturally lazy streak inside her. They're inside me too but mine are less faint.

I was still in bed when my mum knocked on my bedroom door and then barged straight in and said, 'Lottie, can you make sure you're up and about in good time today because we've got a guest joining us for lunch.'

I counted to three in my head and then I said, 'Can I have a million pounds if I correctly guess who it is?'

'Nope,' said my mum. 'Because it's another two weeks until I get paid and I think you know full well who it is. It's Steve.'

'Really?' I said, looking surprised. 'I'm gobsmacked. I honestly thought you were going to say Puff Daddy or Prince Charles.'

My mum frowned. Then she sat on the edge of my bed and crossed her arms moodily in front of her. I watched her from the corner of my eye. Despite the fed-up face, she looked quite small and fragile like that – sitting there defensively like a hunched-up hedgehog. She looked like me.

For a moment or two neither of us said anything. Then my mum said, 'I can't go on forever like this – walking on eggshells around you.'

I looked at her suspiciously. For a second, I was almost tempted to ask her if, on the sly, she was also seeing my RE teacher, Mr Davies. I didn't though because I'm too young to die. Instead, I said, 'Who said anything about eggshells? No one needs to be walking on eggshells around me. I'm helluva tolerant.' And then I think I went a bit red.

'All I'm asking,' said my mum very slowly, 'is that you . . . give . . . him . . . a . . . chance.'

'Hmmm,' I said.

My mum sighed. 'What's *hmmm* supposed to mean?'

'It means *I will*,' I said, feeling slightly annoyed. 'Just stop making such a great big deal out of it.' And then I got out of my bed and stormed off to the bathroom.

I stayed in the shower for ages. I was still feeling a bit annoyed. Not with my mum, but with myself. To be honest, I was shocked and extremely disappointed by how close I'd come to forgetting my freshly made vows of tolerance and understanding. I'd let my mum down. I'd let Mr Davies down. But most of all, I'd let myself down. It didn't feel great.

To make the situation better, I decided to dye my hair. Until this morning, I have been sporting Melody Midnight Ultra Black which is quite shiny and nice but does tend to make me look like a goth. Also, it clashes in a very big way with my naturally beige colouring and when my roots start peeking through, I can easily be mistaken for somebody who is follically challenged. Like this.

This is not really the look I am striving to achieve. Turning off the water, I stepped out of the shower, wrapped myself in a towel and opened the bathroom cabinet. On my shelf, there were three boxes of Melody hair colorant all waiting for their big moment. Dripping a little, I pulled the boxes out of the cupboard and crouched down by the radiator to make an important decision. I needed something to give me confidence. Something that would show Stevie Wonder I had a mind of my own. Something that would prove to the world, once and for all, that I am definitely a **Type A** person!

There was blatantly only one option. The Melody Ice Queen Blue had been kicking around on my shelf for quite a while. Buying that kind of shade is easy but finding the courage to actually *use* it is a different thing altogether. Suddenly feeling totally reckless, I opened up the box, mixed together the contents of the two bottles inside and slopped the whole lot on to my head.

I wish now that I had read the instructions carefully. If I had, I'd have seen this.

Important

Melody Ice Queen Blue ® hair colorant is <u>not recommended</u> for use on hair which has already been treated with an artificial hair colorant product <u>or</u> on hair which is naturally a darker shade. In these cases, the final colour results are likely to differ drastically from those indicated on the outer packaging.

It's fair to say that I have learned an important lesson in life. The hard way. In fact, it was such an intense learning experience that, for a while, I was unable to do anything at all other than sit quietly in the dark and think about it.

By the time I finally managed to calm down and climb out of my wardrobe, Stevie Wonder was already downstairs with his feet firmly under the table.

My mum was fussing around him and wearing too much make-up. When she saw me, she rushed over and put her arm around me and said, 'Lottie, I'd like you to meet my friend Steve. Steve, this is Lottie.' And then she frowned and said, 'What on earth have you done to your hair, darling? It's grey!'

'Yeah, we've already met,' I said. 'And it's not grey, *darling*. It's more of a tarnished silver.' And then I nodded at Detective Sergeant Stevie Wonder and said, 'All right?'

Stevie Wonder stood up and stepped forward to shake my hand. 'Really pleased to meet you, Lottie,' he said. And then with a big cheesy grin, he added, 'Your mum never stops talking about you.'

I gave my mum a deliberately dirty look and shook his hand. It felt a bit weird. I don't think I've ever actually shaken anyone's hand before. I don't really like it.

The timer on the oven tinged. My mum walked over to it, opened the oven door and pulled out a massive home-made pizza. We never ever have home-made pizza. We only eat frozen ones. I think my mum guessed I was about to tell Stevie Wonder this because, before I could even open my mouth, she blurted out, 'So tarnished silver is the latest look, is it?'

I sighed. 'I dunno. I don't actually *care* what the latest look is. I'm not following the crowd – I'm just doing my own thing.'

'Oh,' said my mum. And then she said, 'It's certainly a look that you can grow into. In another forty years, it will look just right.'

Stevie Wonder said, 'Leave her alone, Carolyn.' Then he grinned and winked at me and said, 'Ignore her. I understand the look you're going for, Lottie. My daughter, Lois, is a goth as well.' And then he put his head on one side and said, 'Or is she an emo? I can't remember now. But it's definitely one or the other.'

For a second, I stared at him in horror. The idea of . . .

   a)   being classified as a goth

   b)   being classified as an emo

   or

c) being mentioned in the same sentence as Lanky Lois

. . . was so completely appalling that I was actually speechless. This doesn't happen to me very often. But then, almost before my brain could even register what my mouth was doing, I smirked. I didn't mean to – I just couldn't help it. For some reason, there is just something utterly hilarious about people over the age of thirty using words like goth and emo. It sounds totally desperate. I'd even go as far as to say it sounds bloody stupid.

I started laughing.

Stevie Wonder laughed too. My mum smiled a bit but in that dangerous way which is secretly saying, 'Don't you dare show me up!'

Remembering my manners, I put my hand over my mouth to help keep the rest of my hysterics inside. 'Sorry, Sergeant Giles,' I said, 'I was just—'

'Call me Steve,' said Stevie Wonder.

'Sorry *Steven*,' I said, 'I was just laughing because I'm not actually *either* of those things. I'm not anything. I'm just Lottie Biggs.' And then, because the conversation was so weird and the situation was so intense, I started laughing again. I honestly didn't mean anything rude by it, I just couldn't help it.

Stevie Wonder grinned back at me and nodded approvingly. Then he said, 'That sounds like the best way to me. Just be yourself. Good for you!'

And then my mum banged three plates of home-made pizza on to the kitchen table and we all sat down and ate some, and the rest of the afternoon went pretty smoothly, I thought. My mum flirted with Stevie. Stevie flirted with my mum. And I showed them both how to play *Kick-boxing Queen* on my games console and happily kicked Stevie Wonder repeatedly in the head for over an hour and we all had a really good laugh about it. I even achieved a personal high score.

To be fair to him, Stevie isn't actually as bog awful as I thought. On a scale of one to five with one being only very mildly minging and five being UTTERLY PUTRID, I'd say he's probably only just past number two.

He's certainly not worth breaking any eggs over.

Part 2

a temPOrarY INterruPtION tO the GeNeraL ONwarD fLOw Of mY stream Of CONsCIOusNess Narratlve

Dear Reader,

It has become necessary for me to press the Pause button on my life and to take a moment to consider the overall bigger picture. This is for two reasons. The first of those reasons is that if I don't step away from my problematic personal circumstances and put things back into some kind of sensible perspective, there's a very real danger that my brain will blow up. Blake, my counsellor, once said to me that whenever I feel the murky mists of mayhem muddying my mind, I should try to remove myself as quickly as possible to a place where I feel safe and comfortable, and engage my head with a calming, focused activity. So I've come up to my bedroom and switched on my computer so I can do some writing. But I can't write about the usual stuff. Not now. Because the usual stuff is Gareth and Goose and school and home. The usual stuff is my mum. And more than anything in the world, right now, I especially can't write about her.

So I've switched my computer on and I'm just letting my fingers move freely across the keyboard. And it's really very interesting and liberating because I don't actually know what I'm going to write about next. And the truth is that so long as it keeps my mind off HER and HIM – not to mention the sheMO[17] – I don't exactly care.

And while I'm writing this random stuff, I can pretend that none of the crap that's happening to me actually matters. And, anyway, when you think about what René Descartes said, none of it does matter. Because, in the great big scheme of things, *I* am the only thing that definitely, undoubtedly exists.

But then again, if *I* am the only thing that definitely, undoubtedly exists, why am I even bothering to write all this stuff? I don't need to explain myself to anyone because nobody is ever going to read what I've written! The reader I'm addressing doesn't exist.

OMG, I've just had a totally terrifying thought.

What if Descartes is actually right? I've never really considered the full implications of this before but now I am and I'm finding it completely scary. I mean seriously seriously scary. In fact, it's freaking me out even more than the witch on the swing did in that weird film at the Ponty-Carlo.

Because if the only thing that definitely and undoubtedly exists is me, this means that Goose and Gareth and my mum and Ruthie and Winnie the chinchilla and Blake the

---

[17] Female emo. Obviously.

counsellor quite possibly don't exist. Quite possibly, I've made the whole lot up. They are nothing more than freaky figments of my weird imagination.

OH MY GIDDY GOLDFISH!

I am completely on my own.

But hang on a minute! At the very least, I know that Goose exists. She must do. I have the evidence! On several occasions, Goose has told me that she is an Existentialist Absurdist. Goose thinks that this means her life is essentially absurd. In actual fact, being an Existentialist Absurdist is a lot more complicated than that. I've looked it up on the internet and it made my brain cells boggle just trying to get my head around it all. But basically it's got something to do with the universe being a load of old hogwash. Beyond our own existence, there is nothing else out there. *We* are the only ones responsible for what we do and how we feel, and it's totally pointless trying to find meaning in a meaningless world.

This is not making me feel any better. But . . . BUT . . . it does prove that Goose exists because it proves that she thinks!

I think, therefore I am.

Goose thinks she is an Existentialist Absurdist, therefore she is!

Unless, of course, I just *think* that she thinks this. But what if Goose exists only in my head and *I'm* the one who has decided that Goose has Existential Absurdist tendencies?

SNAKES ON A PLANE!

That leaves me on my own again.

And . . .

oh my giddy grief!

. . . If Goose is nothing more than a creation of my mind – how can I be sure that I'm not simply a weird creation of *someone else's mind*?

Huh???

Perhaps I'm actually nothing more than a drippy character in some random novel and there are loads of people, right at this very second, laughing at me because I think I'm an actual living human person!

This subject is wigging me out so much that I'm going to stop thinking about it immediately and move on to the second reason why I've pressed the pause button.

And that's because I want to explain my decision to divide my *Random Reflections and Philosophical Thoughts* document into two separate parts. When I began writing this thing, I had no intention of organizing my words in this manner. To be honest, I'm surprised I've stuck with it for so long and got this far. But I *have* stuck with it and now I need to mark a significant milestone in my experience as a writer.

EVERYTHING WRITTEN BEFORE THIS POINT WAS WRITTEN BY A NORMAL PERSON

And everything written from here onward will feature the disturbed and desperate outpourings of someone who has just discovered that they could well be spending Christmas Day trapped in a house with Stevie flipping Wonder and Lanky Lois.

And now I've got a third reason for slashing my work into two parts. And it's surely got to be the most crucial reason of all.

I've left home.

A lot has happened since I last did any writing.

A LOT.

So much that it actually makes my brain boggle when I try to get my head round it all.

But I'll start by saying that I am no longer an official resident of 62 Springfield Place, Whitchurch, Cardiff, Wales, United Kingdom, Europe, Planet Earth, The Universe.

Because I've walked out.

Everything I wrote before was written in *a vibrant young city awash with opportunities to immerse oneself in fun, food and Welsh culture*[18] and everything from here onward is being typed in *the hum-drum industrial border town of* Wrexham – where I'm now living with my dad. It's a long and traumatic story and it all starts with a conversation I had with my mum over breakfast on Sunday morning. That was only two days ago and yet it feels like an entire millennium has passed me by since then.

---

[18] This is how Cardiff is described in my dad's travel guide.

We'd got on OK after Stevie's lunch visit the day before. He'd left our house some time in the middle of the afternoon, and me and my mum had gone out for a drive to the Shopping Village to have a mosey around and to check out the special offers.

By the time we got there, it was snowing a bit and freezing cold. Even so, it was quite nice because the Fron Male Voice Choir had swung down all the way from North Wales and were giving a free carol concert in the main arcade. Although I don't normally like listening to that kind of thing, I have to admit that it was definitely helluva festive. At one point, I had a nasty shock though. In the window of one of the shops was a massive poster, and on that massive poster were massive letters which said, ONLY FOURTEEN SHOPPING DAYS LEFT UNTIL CHRISTMAS! For a moment, this completely freaked me out. For one thing, I hadn't actually bought any presents[19] and for another thing, I still had no clue where I was going to be on Christmas Day. I'd spoken to my dad on the phone once or twice but, even though I'd tried to steer the subject in a Christmassy direction, he still hadn't mentioned it.

And then afterwards we drove over to Goose's house and picked her up and took her back to our house where we ordered a Chinese takeaway and watched *Free Willy 4* on DVD. Me and Goose had both seen it five times already and

---

[19] I STILL haven't and now there are only TEN days left!

could speak all the lines before the actors did but my mum hadn't seen it. She's not a very good person to watch a film with, to be honest. She constantly looks confused and says stuff like 'Shhhhh, we're missing what they're saying' every three seconds.

And then Goose went home and I went to bed and then it was Sunday so I got up again and my mum made me fried eggs and bacon for my breakfast – which is one of my all-time favourite things to eat in the whole wide world – and I kissed my mum on her cheek and got myself some orange juice and everything was going all hunky-dory and hokey-cokey and A-OK until she said . . .

'I've been thinking about what we might do on Christmas Day this year.'

I froze, my fists clenching tightly around my knife and fork. And then I put my cutlery down, nervously sipped a little orange juice to buy myself a few seconds, and then, eventually, said, 'But I'm not sure yet what *I'm* doing this Christmas.'

My mum looked surprised. And then her face clouded over and she looked very obviously rather hurt. I felt terrible.

My mum said, 'Have you got some other plans?'

I started fiddling with the end of my fork. 'Well . . . yes,' I said. And then, 'No . . . not yet. But it's dad's turn to see me this year, isn't it?'

My mum's face darkened a little more. 'So he's asked you up there and nobody's bothered to inform me. Thank you very much.'

'No,' I said quickly. 'You know I'd always tell you what's going on. I'm just not sure myself yet.'

'So he *hasn't* asked you?' said my mum.

'No,' I replied uncomfortably. 'I think he's definitely going to though because it's his turn.'

My mum frowned and looked me right in the eye. I don't like it when people look me right in the eye. Except for Gareth. It makes me feel all agitated and harassed. Thumping my elbows on to the table, I rested my jaw in my hand and scowled down at my untouched bacon and eggs.

My mum said, 'Go and ring him now and find out what's going on.'

'No,' I said.

'Well, why not? You want to know what you're doing, don't you?'

My bacon was still steaming but less than it had been at the start of this conversation. It needed eating up. My two egg yolks were yellow and round and perfect.

'I don't want to ring him,' I said. I was starting to feel a bit panicky. It was a very bizarre situation to be in. I *did* want to know what was going on, but I totally did *not* want to ring him and ask. I'm not really sure why.

My mum sighed and then, after a very long pause, she said, 'Do you want *me* to ring him?'

'No,' I said quickly. I hate it when my mum and dad speak to each other. It usually results in a total communication breakdown followed by urgent peace talks.

There was another long silence. Then, very gently, my

mum said, 'If he hasn't said anything to you about going up there and you won't phone and ask him and you won't let *me* phone and ask him, then I suppose you'll just have to stay here with me. But that's not really so bad, is it?'

Still staring at my eggs and bacon, I shook my head. I wasn't lying. It *wasn't* that bad at all. Me and my mum and Ruthie always have an excellent time at Christmas. But I just thought I'd be seeing my dad.

My mum said, 'And you could always see if Gareth wants to join us for tea.'

I started to smile a bit.

My mum said, 'Anyway, I was hoping there'd be quite a crowd of us this year. Ruthie is going to be bringing Michel. And maybe if you're staying, Gareth will come over. And you know I just couldn't do without you, Lottie. It's never the same when you're not here.'

I smiled a lot then.

And then my mum said, 'And I'm also thinking of asking Steve and Lois over.'

I stopped smiling. 'WHAT?'

My mum looked worried. 'Don't be like that, Lottie. I thought you and Steve got on really well yesterday. And you loved playing that *Kick-boxing Queen* game with him. Don't say you didn't because I could see it on your face.'

My fist had clenched around my fork again. I was applying so much pressure to it that I'm surprised the thing didn't snap.

Trying really hard to keep my voice at a normal volume

level, but failing, I said, 'Yeah, but I didn't think he'd be gatecrashing Christmas, did I?'

My mum said, 'He won't be gatecrashing anything. I'm inviting him. Just like I'm inviting Gareth and Michel.'

'Yeah,' I said, 'but why have you got to go and invite *her*?'

'Do you mean Lois?' asked my mum. Pointlessly.

'Yeah. Why does she have to come with him?'

My mum gave me a long, hard look. I'd say it was pretty much a Grade One Stare of Death, to be honest. And then she said, 'Because she's got nowhere else to go. If I invite Steve over – and I plan to – then of course I'll invite Lois to come with him. Because her mum's dead, Lottie.'

I hadn't expected her to say this.

I opened my mouth to say something and then – because I couldn't think of anything *to* say, I started to cry. But it wasn't a *good* let-it-all-out, head-clearing cry – it was an absolutely pig-awful, rotten-as-rotting-rhubarb cry. Tears were streaming down my face and I knew that they were selfish and stupid and terrible tears. But also, they were angry and trapped tears too because if my dad had invited me up to Wrexham like he should have done in the first place, then none of this would have mattered anyway. A big fat tear ran straight down my cheek and plopped on to one of my untouched egg yolks. My head felt a bit funny. As I stared at the egg yolk, it sneered at me through a pair of yellow-tinted cyber-goggles and said, 'Deal with it!'

I said, 'Yeah, but it's not *my* fault her mum's dead, is it?' And then I slammed my fork down on to both my egg yolks and made them explode all over the tablecloth.

I only caught a tiny glimpse of my mum's face as I stormed out of the kitchen. She looked shocked by my behaviour and – what was worse – she looked disgusted.

I don't blame her. Somewhere, underneath this massive rage which had completely hijacked my head, I was feeling totally and utterly shocked and disgusted by my behaviour too.

twO's COmPaNY . . .

I'm not sure what happened next. I remember going up to my room and typing away furiously on the computer but then I lost track of time. Most people lose hats and homework and occasionally – if they're really careless – their iPods and phones, but on Sunday I completely lost track of an entire couple of hours. Or rather, there was so much stuff buzzing about between my ears that everything stopped making proper sense and I've got no clear idea of the specific order of events. One second I was writing about the pointlessness of trying to find meaning in a meaningless world and the next thing I knew I was sitting on a bench on the traffic island in the middle of Whitchurch village. And I honestly for the life of me can't remember exactly how I got there.

But there I was.

Just sitting on a bench.

Like this.

---

[20] Well, not ACTUALLY like this! I was wearing my jeans for a start. But this is a good visual approximation of the MOOD I was in. In making this illustration I have been helped by the famous French artist Henri de Toulouse-Lautrec (1864–1901). My art teacher showed us all a documentary about him once. As long as I live, I'll never EVER forget the first words of that film. They were these: *Although Henri de Toulouse-Lautrec was only five feet tall, he was not a small man; he had an enormously large manhood.*

148

And while I was sitting there, the inside of my head was whizzing round and round with stuff like this:

You CAN'T Make Me spend Christmas Day with Loopy Lois and Stevie Flipping Wonder... OH MY GIDDY GRIEF! I'm going upstairs... I think therefore I write... I write therefore I am and what I am... is all ALONE!... so Deal with it! and what I am and what I am... WHAT IS GOING ON?

And it's perfectly possible that I might have sat in a dizzy trance on that stupid public bench forever – if Elvis Presley hadn't decided to join me. He had his traffic cone with him. It was pointed straight at my ear.

Believe me, it's hard to remain in a dizzy trance

when someone is sitting right next to you and singing straight down a traffic cone and into your ear.

I don't know whether he was using the cone as an amplifier by touching it with his lips and causing it to vibrate *or* if the sound energy was just being used more efficiently because it was all concentrated in one specific direction – but I do know that it was extremely loud. And suddenly, something in my brain popped back into gear and all the random stuff was swept out of my head until I was left with one single very clear thought:

What the blinking heck am I doing here?

And this was a very refreshing thought to have because it proved without any shadow of doubt that I existed.

When Elvis had finished his song, he said, 'That one's called *All Shook Up*. I chose it especially for you, little lady, because, if you don't mind me saying, you're looking a bit shook up yourself.'

'I *am* all shook up,' I said.

'Anything I can help you with?' asked Elvis.

'I doubt it,' I said.

'Why don't you try telling your Uncle Elvis all about it?' said Elvis.

I thought about this for a second and then shook my head and said, 'It's just everything about my life . . . It's way too complicated.'

Elvis laughed. 'It's a common enough problem. You ask

most people and they'll tell you their lives are complicated. It's all part of life's rich tapestry.'

I felt a tear escape. Frustrated, I wiped it away with the palm of my hand. 'My life isn't a rich tapestry though,' I said. 'It's just one great big massive mountain of nutty knots.'

Elvis frowned and drummed his fingers thoughtfully against his traffic cone. Then he said, 'What you got to do is examine the knots. Then choose one that looks like it might be a bit looser than the rest and try sorting that one out first. If you keep doing that, bit by bit, it should all straighten out and fall into place.'

'But I don't want to examine the stupid knots,' I said.

Elvis shrugged. 'You ever heard of Socrates?'[21]

'Socra-who?' I said. I was starting to get a bit irritated for some reason.

'Socrates,' said Elvis. 'Greek bloke. Did a lot of thinking. Well, he reckoned that *the unexamined life is not worth living.*'

I stood up. I don't know why but I was now well and truly agitated. Every single atom of my existence felt like it was a highly stressed-out component part of some great big squirming lump of agitated agitation. Even my grey hair felt agitated. I glared at Elvis and, before I could stop myself, I snapped, 'So now you're a flipping counsellor as well as a

---

[21] I looked him up on the computer in Wrexham library. He's another one whose name isn't spelled how it sounds. Think cream teas, lemon teas, sockra-teas.

philosopher and an Elvis impersonator, are you?'

Elvis looked a bit startled for a moment but then he laughed. 'No,' he said. 'I apologize. I ain't a counsellor, am I? I'm a brown-eyed handsome man and my mission is to ensure that there's a whole lotta shakin' goin' on in the centre of Whitchurch. And, to be honest, it's high time I had a little less conversation and got on with it.' And then he picked up his traffic cone and started singing another scatty song to me and whoever else happened to be passing. But mostly he sang it to himself.

'I've had enough of this,' I said and started walking very quickly up the main street in the direction of the bus stop. As I walked, my breath froze in the air around me, making me look like some kind of weird walking volcano which was about to erupt. To be honest, that's pretty much how I felt too – except that I was extremely cold and volcanoes are usually extremely hot. I crossed my arms around me and jammed my hands under my armpits to try to get some feeling back into my fingers, which had gone almost completely numb. Behind me, Elvis continued to sing. Even though I was still incredibly agitated, I was already wishing I hadn't been so arsey with him. I don't know why I'd been so arsey with him because he didn't in the least bit deserve it. I suppose the truth is that I just couldn't help myself. I was in an extremely arsey mood.

When I reached the bus stop, I stopped and leaned against the side of the brand new shelter, which had only been placed there a couple of weeks earlier. My fingers, still jammed into my pits, weren't feeling the least bit warmer. In fact, they felt far more like the frozen fish variety of finger than they did the human type. I wiggled them to check they could still move and once I was satisfied that they actually could, I thumped my head back against the glass and stared into space. And then I rubbed my eyes and did a double take. Because I had seen The Truth. It was written in marker pen right across the new glass.

WE ALL NEED HELP!

I stood and thought about this for quite some time. I couldn't decide whether it made me feel better or worse to know that everybody else was just as hopeless and as miserable as I was. In the end, I decided that it definitely made me feel worse so I turned to face another direction in order to look at something else.

On another of the brand new glass panels, the same person had written:

WE ARE ON ARE OWN

It was a very existential thing to write. It wasn't absurd. But it was very depressing. And all of a sudden, right there, by myself at the bus stop, I began to cry. And I mean really cry. I'm not talking about the odd leaky tear that I could quickly brush away with the back of my hand – I'm talking about the full force of the Niagara Falls streaming down my face and creating puddles on the ground. I think I might actually have even been making a boo-hoo sound.

A bus pulled up. Quickly, I stared down at my feet so that nobody on it would spot that I was boo-hooing. After a moment or two, a voice shouted, 'Are you getting on this bus then?'

I stared more intently at my shoes and hoped nobody would notice me.

'Oi . . . Lady with the prematurely grey hair . . . Do you want this bus or not?'

With a jolt, I realized the bus driver was shouting at *me*. I unfolded my arms, wiped my eyes quickly with a couple of frozen fish fingers and shouted back, 'Not.' And then I added, 'I can stand here if I want to, can't I?'

The driver looked annoyed and muttered something. Then the doors closed with a hiss, and he and the bus pulled away and disappeared in the direction of town. And this made me feel even sadder than I'd actually felt before because I knew then that – more than anything else in the entire world – I wanted to be on that bus. And I wanted to be going somewhere much further than the city centre. I wanted to be going far, far away from Cardiff. And from my mum. And Stevie Wonder. And Lois. Especially from Lois. Who doesn't have a mum.

'Lottie! Are you OK?'

Another voice made me look up. This time, with a huge rush of relief, I saw it was Goose. She was on her way to her shift at the Ponty-Carlo Sunday Morning Cinema Club. I could see a little of her atrocious electric blue and yellow uniform peeping out from beneath the bottom of her coat. With big worried eyes, she said, 'Are you OK?' And then she said, 'Cool hair!'

It's a really weird thing but sometimes when I'm feeling utterly miserable, the sound of a kind and concerned voice saying kind and concerned things to me just pushes me totally and truly over the edge and makes me go all wobbly like a jelly baby. On other occasions, though, I'm just downright rude and arsey – like I was with Elvis. I'll admit that this makes me a very difficult and unpredictable human person to be around.

Instead of giving Goose a proper answer, I wobbled like a jelly baby and started boo-hooing even louder.

Goose looked alarmed. 'Lottie, what the heck is the matter?'

I shut my eyes and tried to think of a way to explain. But I was so cold that it was hard to concentrate. And it was way too difficult to explain anyway. So many things were the matter that I didn't even know where to begin. I opened my eyes and made a big frustrated sound that went something like this:

Ooooooofffffff

. . . and then I jerked my head at the two stupid pieces of graffiti on the brand new panels of glass and said, rather lamely, 'Well, they aren't helping much for a start!'

Goose turned and looked. And then she frowned and said, 'I see what you mean. That's well depressing, isn't it?'

'Yeah,' I said. 'Yeah, it is. Well depressing and well sad. I mean . . . I used to think our English teacher, Mr Wood, was a total tragic weirdo for getting so wound up about missing apostrophes and rubbish grammar and everything . . . but when I look at that stupid graffiti written there, I can absolutely understand where he's coming from. I mean, honestly, Goose, it makes me sick. It really does. Why go to the lengths of ruining a perfectly good bus shelter if you can't even be bothered to learn the difference between are and our?' And then I thumped my head as hard as I could against the glass. It must have been that special reinforced stuff because it didn't budge an inch. The pain that shot through my brain made me almost scream though. 'Shit,' I whispered, and clutched hold of my forehead.

Goose put her hands to her head and said, 'STOP IT,' and gave me a blatantly odd look.

After a moment of total silence, she added, 'Oh my God! Is that honestly why you're so upset?'

'Well . . .' I said, still clutching my throbbing forehead and choking back a sob, '. . . that's not the whole reason.'

'Oh,' said Goose and nodded. She looked a bit relieved.

And then, before I even knew that I was going to say it, I grabbed hold of her arm and said, 'Goose, can you lend me some money?'

Goose frowned down at my hand on her arm and then slowly she took her bag off her shoulder. It wasn't her usual kind of bag – it was one I'm pretty sure I'd never seen before. It appeared to be some kind of scruffy old briefcase with a long leather shoulder strap. Most people wouldn't be able to get away with a bag like that but Goose can because she's a Type A, Master of Fashion.

She must also be a bit of a mind-reader because her face reddened and she said, 'Yeah, yeah, I know it's a bit *last season* to be bothering with a bag but my coat pockets just aren't big enough. Whereas this old thing's got helluva storage. Tim at work – did I mention that he's doing A levels in Film Studies, Psychology and Media? – well, he reckons that stylish and efficient baggage is the pathway to organizational harmony.' Then she frowned at me again and said, 'Where's your coat?'

And suddenly I realized why I was so completely cold. 'I forgot it,' I said. 'And I forgot my purse; that's why I'm asking to borrow some money.'

Goose narrowed her eyes and looked at me suspiciously.

For a moment, I thought she was actually morphing into my mum or something. But then, in her reassuringly familiar Goosey voice, she said, 'What d'you need it for?'

'To get away from here,' I said.

Goose began to chew her thumbnail and looked at me for a long time. Eventually she said, 'Yeah, but . . . like . . . when you say away from *here* . . . what does that mean in terms of *where* specifically?'

Goose is so wordy sometimes. It's totally unnecessary. 'Look,' I said. 'I know . . . yeah . . . that you're just trying to look out for my interests . . . and I totally respect and appreciate you for that . . . but . . . the thing is . . . . I'm in quite a majorly intense situation right now . . . and the only thing that would make it feel fractionally less intense would be if . . . well . . . . I just really need to go and see my sister Ruthie . . . but she lives in Aberystwyth . . . and I haven't currently got access to any money . . . so . . . well . . . I really need to lend some off you.'

For the billionth time, Goose frowned. I think I did too. To be honest, the news that I wanted to see my sister had caught me by surprise. I hadn't even bothered to tell myself first. Goose scratched her head thoughtfully and then she said, '*Borrow*.'

'Huh?' I said.

'*You* want to borrow money. You want *me* to lend it.'

I looked at Goose in amazement and then I said, '*Lend . . . borrow . . .* who flipping cares? They're only poxy words. Oh my giddy grief! Since when have you been an English teacher?' And then — because I really totally did want to borrow/lend some money from her — I got a grip of myself and said, 'Look, I'm sorry, Goose, I didn't mean to have a pop at you but I'm really uptight at the moment.'

Goose said, 'Flipping Norah! You don't say!'

'I'm sorry,' I muttered.

'Why can't you ask your mum?' asked Goose.

'I can't,' I said in a panic. 'We are so totally not speaking at the moment.'

Goose began to chew her other thumbnail and continued to look worried. 'Ruthie will be home for Christmas next week anyway, won't she? Why d'you need to go and see her now?'

'I just do,' I said. I was starting to feel really desperate — like I could hardly breathe.

Goose's eyes narrowed. For several seconds, she just stood there, staring at me, with her super-scary skinny-fit eyes.

To be honest, I'm surprised she could actually see anything. I must have looked like this:

After another massive tense silence, Goose said, 'You're running away, aren't you?'

I turned away from her, leaned my forehead against the panel of glass, which was telling me that WE ARE ON ARE OWN and thought about this question carefully. After a moment or two, I said, 'I'm just removing myself from a difficult situation.'

'No you're not – you're running away,' said Goose.

'*Please*, Goose . . .' My voice was now little more than a croaky whisper. 'I really, *really* need your help.' And then I started to cry again. I couldn't keep it inside any longer.

Goose just stood there looking uncomfortable. In the distance, further up the high street, I could see another bus making its way towards us. That thing about buses coming along in threes is totally true. 'Please, Goose,' I said again. I was *really* desperate. I'd have got down on my knees and begged if I thought it would have made any difference.

'But what about your mum?' said Goose.

'She hates me anyway,' I said. I shivered uncomfortably and looked away so that Goose couldn't see my face. I think that, deep down, I knew this wasn't *technically* true but my brain had stopped worrying about hard facts and was kind of making things up as it went along. And really, all I could properly focus on was the approaching bus, which was getting closer and closer. 'I just want to see my sister,' I said.

Goose looked up the street towards the oncoming bus. Then she frowned and chewed her lip. Then she looked up at the bus again. It was now only a few seconds away from reaching us. Goose's frown deepened. She chewed her lip a little more. I waited, so anxious that I was actually holding my breath.

'OK, I'll lend you the money to get to Aberystwyth,' she said. 'But on two conditions. One, you phone your mum and let her know where you—'

'I haven't got my—'

'And two,' said Goose, cutting me off before I could finish, 'I'm coming with you.' And then she added, 'Anyway, two's company.'

I stared at her. My brain couldn't believe what my ears had just heard.

'You're coming with me?' I repeated stupidly.

'Have you got a problem with that?' asked Goose. She sounded quite annoyed.

'No,' I whispered. And then, not for the first time in my life, I threw my arms around my best friend in the whole world and gave her a really massive tight hug. But this time, I was boo-hooing like a baby all over her shoulder. Goose wrapped her arms around me and hugged me back.

Behind us, there was a hissing noise. Then a voice called, 'Oi . . . Any chance of you two breaking up the lady love and getting on this bus or what?'

Goose gently pushed me away from her and turned round. I did too. Through the open door of the bus, the driver was leaning forward over his ticket dispensing machine and watching us with a big leery grin. He was wearing a cheap Santa hat, but it didn't make him look Christmassy. It made him look like something out of that film *And They Died Screaming*.

'Urrrggghhh . . . Yuck . . . Shut up!' I said.

Goose put her hands on her hips. 'Er . . . *hello*,' she said to the bus driver with a definite hint of annoyance in her voice, '. . . that wasn't *lady love*.' And then she gave me a quick sideways grin and added, 'That was actually a highly touching and emotional moment strictly between me and my sweet soul sister.'

I nodded in agreement and with a small jolt of amazement, I realized that *I* was smiling too.

The pervy Santa driver shrugged. 'Call it what you like but I still calls it lady love. Now, are you getting on my flipping bus or what?'

. . . But three Is a MaGIC NumBer

That all happened on Sunday. It's Tuesday now and I'm a helluva long way from that bus stop in Whitchurch and that dodgy driver with his pervy personal comments.

I'm also a long way away from Goose. And Gareth.

But, hey, that's OK because I'm a long way from my mum and Sexy Steve as well.

Last night, me, Caradoc and my dad watched the film *The Empire Strikes Back*. I've seen it hundreds of times before because my dad is a massive fan of the *Star Wars* trilogy and he usually gets his box set out every time I visit. I don't mind though because I secretly love *Star Wars* too. I love all that Jedi knight versus the dark side stuff and I also love the idea that – when push comes to shove – alien entities, robotic droids and actual human people are capable of cooperating with one another and standing side by side in order to fight the forces of evil. When you think about it, it's as inspiring as Mr Davies' assembly about eggs.

But last night, I'd have probably sat and watched any old rubbish. Even *And They Died Screaming*. To be honest, I was just happy to stare at the TV screen and avoid any pointless conversational chit-chat. Although he hasn't said anything specific, I get the impression that my dad is secretly very peeved about having to take an entire day off work yesterday to drive all the way to Aberystwyth and back. I don't know why I think this – I just do. I suppose it's what is simply known as an intuitive hunch. But then again, it might just be plain old paranoia.

When the film finished, my dad said, 'Brilliant. Cracking. And that's where they should have left it. As a trilogy. Those newer prequel things are a total waste of time. They bring shame on the name of *Star Wars*. But the first three are perfection. Three is a magic number, kids. Remember that.'

Caradoc, who had spent most of the film playing with his PSP, looked up smiling and said, 'Like you, me and Lottie?'

'Yes,' said my dad. 'Or you, me and Mummy.'

I went to bed soon after that. I'm staying in the spare room. It doesn't have a computer in it or any posters on the wall and there isn't a sweet elderly chinchilla living next door but it's nice enough. And I'd had a very tiring day – physically and emotionally – and I just wanted to be by myself.

But my dad's words stayed with me long after my eyes had closed. Because he's right. Three *is* a magic number and there's a shedload of evidence to support this. The number three has a special power that other numbers simply don't have. Three is stronger, brighter and much more interesting than any other dreary old digit. I'd even go so far as to say that, in the right context, three has a rare and mysterious beauty. If this sounds utterly bonkers, consider the facts:

- As my dad rightly stated, *Star Wars* should have remained forever as a trilogy. But then they made three more films so now it is technically a *sixology*. Except that the word *sixology* doesn't actually exist – I just made it up. The truth is that nobody cares what a group of six films is called because six is blatantly not a magic number.

- My favourite food is almost always made up of three vital parts. Take as an example this list quickly compiled off the top of my head:
  - curry, rice and chips
  - bacon, lettuce and tomato sandwich
  - treacle pie, chocolate sauce and ice cream

- My favourite band in the whole world is the Jimi Hendrix Experience. Sadly, they are unable to give live performances today because Jimi no longer exists in this earthly dimension – and, in fact, hasn't since 1970. The Jimi Hendrix Experience comprised three band members: guitar, bass and drums. While together, they produced three classic albums. Perfect.

- One of the first things I ever learned in art is that there are three primary colours: red, yellow and blue. These three colours can be mixed together to create every other single colour in existence. WOW![22]

- There are also three colours on the Welsh flag: red, white and green. Now, I'm not being biased just because I happen to be Welsh but I genuinely and honestly believe that the Welsh flag is the most stylish flag in the entire cosmos. It's certainly the only flag I know that has a rampaging dragon on it. I bet, if forced to undertake a lie-detector test, most English people would actually admit that they wish it was their flag too. To be fair, all the best flags have three colours in them. France has a *tricolor* – not a quadcolor – and so do Ireland, Italy and Holland and loads of other

---

[22] This doesn't include any colours that need shades of black or white in them. But strictly speaking black is not a colour – it is merely an absence of light. And white isn't a colour either – it is merely an absence of darkness. This means that grey is not a colour either. It is merely larkness. Or dight.

places. Incidentally, England's flag has only got two colours on it. Two is not a magic number.

- Mr Wood, my English teacher, is always banging on about something called *the rule of three*. He reckons that it instantly adds a distinct poetic quality to the written word. To demonstrate this, he used the example of Julius Caesar saying *I came, I saw, I conquered* and William Shakespeare's Juliet asking the question *Romeo, Romeo, wherefore art thou Romeo?* At the time, I'm sorry to say that I can distinctly remember muttering, 'Boring, boring, boring' under my breath. Now that I am a little older and wiser, I actually find this quite interesting, interesting, interesting.

In addition to all the above, I've been giving it some further thought and I can conclude with confidence that three is also a magic number in the scientific world of science. Despite the fact that I usually find this subject to be extremely boring, boring, boring, I've had several conversations with Mr Thomas, my double-science teacher, which have been freaky, fascinating and fab. Like the time he told me that polar bears don't have white fur – it's actually transparent. Or the time he told me that if you strap a magnet to a pigeon's head, it will fly around in circles forever. Personally though, I think this would be really cruel. But I don't mind admitting that I've grown to quite like these conversations with Thommo. If – right now – I was in my science classroom asking Mr Thomas his opinion as to whether or not he supports the belief that three is a magic number, I can just imagine that he would raise up his right eyebrow – in a way that doesn't make him look like James Bond – rub his chin thoughtfully and say something along the lines of:

'Well, Lottie, that's an interesting question. Thanks for asking it. *Is* three a magic number? Well . . . not exactly *magic* . . . because that would imply that there is some supernatural force at play and – as a scientist – I believe there's a higher likelihood that everything can be understood by using a rational explanation. But the number three definitely crops up with a surprising frequency. Think about the three states of matter . . . solid, liquid and gas. And then there are the three particles that make up every single thing that you can see – and *can't* see – around you . . . protons, neutrons and electrons. And, hey, let's not forget the three methods by which heat flows . . . conduction, convection and radiation. I suppose too I should mention the three types of rock . . . igneous, sedimentary and metamorphic. I'm sure there are probably other examples. If you want to stay behind for a few minutes after the lesson, we can try to think of some more. Does that adequately answer your question?'

At this point in our imaginary conversation Mr Davies, my RE teacher, randomly pops into the science lab to borrow a test tube that he's going to use as the minaret on his model mosque, organizes his right hand so that it looks as if he's aiming an air dart at me, and says:

'What's this? *Hmmm? Hmmm?* Are we discussing the

divine qualities of the number three? Schlop schlop. Interesting, *hmmm*? Very very interesting. I'm an RE man by trade and the obvious example that springs to mind is the Christian Trinity . . . the father, son and the holy ghost. That's basically three persons existing in *one Godhead*. Just imagine that. *Hmmm?* Then, of course, there are the magi . . . or three wise men . . . who gave gifts to the infant baby Jesus. But we can cast our net wider than Christianity, Lottie. Oh yes we can! Hinduism has the Trimurti . . . or the three great gods, Brahmä, Vishnu and Śhiva . . . . and, if we look to Judaism, we find the three patriarchs . . . Ab, Isaac and Jacob. What do you make of that? *Hmmm?*'

But right now I am *not* in my science lesson. I'm actually in the front room of my dad's little house in Wrexham and I'm using his computer to type up all these thoughts in an attempt to disentangle the mountain of nutty knots in my life. And even though I was dead tired last night, the weird thing is that I don't think I actually slept a single wink – so I've been down here since 5.37 a.m. and it's now almost eight o'clock. Dad is just about to go to work, Sally is flapping around and getting Caradoc ready for school and I'm just sitting here and keeping out of everyone's way. I don't know why though. Deep down, I reckon I could do with their company. After all, I must be feeling fairly lonely if I'm reduced to having an imaginary conversation with two of my teachers from school! It does prove one thing though. It proves that I listen. On more than one occasion, I've been accused – unfairly – of not paying enough attention during my lessons. If any of my teachers were to read the words I've just typed, I think they would be forced to take back their unkind words, give me some proper credit and apologize.

It surely also proves the magnificence of the number three! And if any doubt dares to remain regarding the mysterious, magical and mind-bendingly marvellous qualities of this number, I can banish it forever by simply recalling to my mind a very special meeting that took place on the bus from Whitchurch village to Cardiff Central Bus Station. And I know I'm flitting back and forth through time a bit – but the truth is, logic doesn't always run in a perfectly straight line.

No sooner had me and Goose taken our seats when a shout from the back of the bus caused me to turn round. There on the back seat, looking absolutely sexadelic in his rugby kit, was none other than Gareth David Lloyd George Stingecombe. He had a massive grin on his face and was looking very pleased about life. He shifted a few seats forward to join us and said, 'Lottie! Love the silver hair, babe!' And then he turned to Goose and said, 'Goose!' And then he turned back to me and said, 'You'll never guess what, Lottie, the most amazing thing has happened! And I was going to phone and tell you but I'm all out of credit. Anyway, the thing is . . .' And then he frowned, gazed into my eyes which were still red from all the crying I'd done at the bus stop and said, 'What's the matter?'

I chewed my lip and considered what I should say to him. The whole situation was quite awkward really.

'What is it?' asked Gareth again. He was frowning so hard that his eyebrows had joined together.

Through the window, I could see the buildings getting bigger and the traffic getting thicker as we got closer and closer to the centre of the city. I picked at a loose bit of foam spilling out of a hole on the back of my seat and said, 'Things between me and my mum have reached a crisis point, Gareth. So I'm going to Aberystwyth to spend a few days with Ruthie. Goose is coming with me.'

Gareth looked at Goose and frowned even deeper. 'What, *now*?'

'Yep,' said Goose.

'When are you coming back?'

'I'm not sure,' I said.

Gareth breathed inward and seemed to hold his breath. And then he said, 'Will you be back for the end-of-term disco?'

'I'm not sure,' I said again.

Goose gave me a slightly funny look and said, 'Well, we probably will because *I'm* not missing the end-of-term disco. I can tell you that now.'

Gareth stared at her. 'But you can't be going *now* – you've got your work uniform on!'

Goose just shrugged.

'You can't go,' said Gareth. He had forgotten Goose and was looking straight at me. Right into my eyes. Gareth has got very beautiful green eyes and when I look deeply into them, it's very difficult to keep a clear thought in my head. With a massive effort of inner strength, I pulled myself together. 'I can, Gaz. And I am.'

Gareth took hold of my hands. In a weirdly wobbly – but way too loud – voice, he said, 'But you can't because . . . because . . . I love Ewan McGregor!'

'What?' I said.

'You love Ewan McGregor?' said Goose. 'Random!' And then she started laughing.

'Ewan McGregor,' spluttered Gareth, who had suddenly developed a nasty cough. 'The actor. I love the way he mixes mainstream cinema with independent art-house roles, and I particularly enjoyed his performance as Christian in *Moulin Rouge.'*

'Oh,' I said, slightly confused. 'Thanks for sharing that fact with me.'

The three of us sat in silence for a while. For some reason, it seemed difficult to know quite what to say. Eventually, the bus swung around sharply by the castle and I knew I'd soon have to say an even more difficult goodbye.

Gareth, who had been chewing his knuckles ever since his revelation about Ewan McGregor, suddenly blurted out, 'But you're not even wearing a coat!'

'Neither are you,' I reminded him with a small smile.

Gareth didn't smile back. Instead, he fumbled with the zip of a big sports bag that was resting between his feet and pulled out a thick red training top. 'Put this on,' he said. 'I brought it with me as a spare. I'd rather you wear it.'

My stomach flipped over inside me. Gareth has a way of

making it do that sometimes. In a good way though. Not in a stomach bug kind of way. Gratefully, I took the top from him and held it in my lap, twisting my fingertips through the rough cotton.

'Come on,' said Goose, picking up her briefcase. 'This is where we all get off.' And then she said to Gareth, 'Where are you off to, anyway?'

'Rugby training,' said Gareth. His mouth had turned down at the edges and he looked really miserable.

'In the middle of town?' said Goose.

'Hmm,' said Gareth.

I placed the training top around my shoulders and stood up. 'We've got to go and find the bus to Aberystwyth. Take it easy, yeah, Gaz.' I kept my eyes fixed firmly on the window. I couldn't look at him. I don't know why but I felt like I was letting him down in some way.

At last the bus came to a stop and we all got off. 'Bye then, Gareth,' I said. 'I hope your training session goes well.' And then I frowned and added, 'Why is your training session in the city centre anyway?'

Gareth shrugged his shoulder. 'Oh I dunno. Doesn't matter.'

I knew he was fed up because Gareth hardly ever mutters. He's not the muttering type. I am though. I touched him on the arm and said, 'We'd better be off. See you soon.'

Gareth shook his arm from me and snapped, 'Yeah, but when though?' And I knew then that he was in a seriously bad mood because he's really not the sort of person who'd get all snappy with me.

'Soon,' I promised. And then – because I really hate emotional goodbyes – I squeezed his arm and just turned right round and walked off in the direction of the ticket office. I heard Goose say, 'She'll be OK, Gareth. We're only going to stay with her sister,' and then she caught up with me and threaded her arm through mine.

And that would have been all there is to tell about that gloomy bus trip from Whitchurch village to Cardiff Central Bus Station had it not been for the miraculous thing that happened just afterwards. Gareth's footsteps came thumping over the concrete forecourt and I turned to see him running towards us with his sports bag flung over his shoulder and his face all red and serious-looking. 'Gareth, what are you doing?' I said.

He slowed down to a halt and, sounding slightly cross, he said, 'What do you think I'm doing?'

'I dunno,' I said.

'I'm coming with you, aren't I?' Then, before I could even grasp the full meaning of his words, he said, 'Don't tell me I'm being daft and I can't come with you because I know I'm daft and I'm coming anyway. Coach Jenkins reckons that when you're gonna make a dummy pass on the field of play, two men can just about manage but three is a lot safer.' And with that, he threaded his arm through my spare one and – with no further discussion – we all walked off together to get three tickets to Aberystwyth. Me, Gareth and Goose. And I felt magic.

a PartICuLarLY GreY tuesDaY MOrNING IN wreXham

To be honest, that magic has worn off. It's not easy to feel fantastically magic or special when you're sitting on a wonky chair in a public library and typing on a keyboard that has got crisp crumbs stuck between all the keys. But this is what I've been reduced to. When Sally got back from the school run this morning she made me a cup of coffee and said, 'You can't monopolize that computer all day, Lottie. I need it to see if I've had any new orders. I could be losing customers.' Sally has an online shop selling her own home-made herbal calming remedies. She tried one of her new concoctions out on me once and it tasted like a mixture of liquorice and dust. It made me feel a little bit sick and then it made me want to drink loads of water but it didn't make me feel particularly calm. Mind you, Sally's remedies blatantly don't work because Sally is actually one of the most stressed-out people I've ever encountered in my entire life. Even her hair looks stressed out. It's all tight and frizzy and obviously no one has ever recommended Melody Ultra Soft Conditioning Treatment (for Dry Difficult Hair) to her. And she cries even more than I do. And over silly things – like the dinner being a bit overcooked or other people parking their cars too close to her Nissan Micra. Once, when we all went on holiday to Spain, Sally cried because the sun was too hot! To be fair to her though, she's nice enough. And she did give me a tenner to spend on whatever I want in Wrexham today. And she also lent me her library card. At the time, I'd thought this was a bit of a weird thing to lend me and I hadn't wanted to take it but now I'm really glad I did because it's pouring with rain outside and Sally asked me not to come back to the house until four o'clock. She's a very busy person.

I've been to Wrexham loads of times but I've never really noticed until today how totally dark the sky is. It's much darker than I'm used to. This morning it looked like this:

Even at 10 a.m. There was hardly enough daylight to give the world any colour and, for a while, I felt like I was trapped in one of those weird black and white films that Tim Overup gets so excited about. It made me very claustrophobic, if I'm honest, and this is unusual for me because I'm actually someone who enjoys sitting inside my own wardrobe.

For a while I just followed my feet around the town centre. Lots of the shops were empty and buried behind plywood boards and fly-posters. In another shop window, the glass had been entirely covered with identical posters that said:

QUALITY GOOD'S END OF LINE'S OUTLET

. . . and this made me smile at first because it made me think of how my English teacher, Mr Wood, would have needed one of Sally's herbal rescue remedies if he'd seen this abominable abuse of apostrophes. But then it also got me thinking about school and about Goose and Gareth and I stopped smiling then and just felt really flat.

And then it started to rain and I swear to God that the raindrops were fatter and colder than they ever are in Cardiff. I was wearing a parka which Ruthie had given me and – even though it's two sizes too big for me and smells of mud – I was really glad I *was* wearing it because those raindrops felt like they'd been dumped on my head directly from the North Pole. Right now, Ruthie's parka is drying on the back of my chair and I'm really grateful it's there because it's warm and snugly and smells like a slightly smelly friend.

To escape the rain, I ducked into a shop. It wasn't the nearest shop – that was actually a branch of Vogue Marché which sells smock-tops and slacks for the more mature lady – but it was the nearest shop to me which looked like it might have something interesting inside. It was called:

I pushed open the door and stepped in, out of the rain. The shop was massive. Every inch of every wall was covered in racks and racks of tightly-pressed-together *stuff*. In fact, there was so much stuff in there that my brain needed a few seconds to digest it all. Not only were there Doug's videos and discs but there were also DVDs, computer games, ancient LPs, tape cassettes, comic books, old games consoles . . . There was probably other stuff too, which I never even spotted. By anyone's standards, it was an extremely interesting shop. A few people who looked like they were in their twenties or thirties were slowly browsing the shelves with frowns of total and utter concentration on their faces and I noticed, with a jolt of surprise and pleasure, that most of them were wearing parkas too. I'm not sure why this made me feel so good exactly. But it did.

Shoving my hands into the pockets of Ruthie's parka, I wandered over to a rack of films and started looking at the titles on offer. Behind the desk, a man with a young face but hair as grey as mine put down a screwdriver that he was using to fix a prehistoric computer and said to me, 'Shouldn't you be in school, love?'

'No,' I said. 'I'm on holiday at my dad's.'

The man behind the counter – Doug? – nodded suspiciously. 'Sorry, sweetheart, I have to ask. I get every ragamuffin in Wrexham in here otherwise.'

I smiled and turned back to the films. There was lots of stuff I'd never heard of and there was lots of stuff with foreign titles too. I looked to see if they had that film *And They Died Screaming*, but they didn't – which was just as well because I wouldn't ever have bought it anyway. I wanted to buy something though. I really did. So I scanned the racks of films again and I found a film called *Forrest Gump,* and just seeing the cover made me smile because it was a title that I recognized, and for some reason that made me instantly happy.

The bell on the shop door tinkled. Two boys, who looked like they were probably in Year 9, walked in and joined me by the films. From the counter, the man who I was soon to discover *was* called Doug said, 'Shouldn't you lads be in school?'

'Nah,' said one of the boys, 'We both got to go to the dentist's in an hour.'

Doug looked at the two boys doubtfully and said, 'What?

Both of you? And weren't you at the dentist's last week?'

'Yeah,' said the boy who'd spoken before, 'I suffer chronic with my teeth. We both do as it happens. I'm having a couple of molars out today to make a little space at the back and what are you having done, Jay?'

The other boy who was blatantly called Jay put his hand against his jaw and said, 'Root canal treatment.'

Doug nodded suspiciously. 'Sorry, lads. Gotta ask. You know how it is.'

'I do, Doug, I do,' said the first boy. 'You'd get every ragamuffin in Wrexham in here otherwise.'

Doug gave the boys another doubtful look and then shrugged and turned his attention back to the ancient computer.

I stood still with the copy of *Forrest Gump* in my hands and had another quick look around to see if there was anything else I might want to buy. Next to me, from the corner of my eye, I could see Jay and his friend whispering and giggling. They both seemed very preoccupied with the titles placed high up on the wall above all our heads. A quick, darting movement made me turn and look at them properly. Jay's friend was clutching a DVD in his hand and the two of them were fixed intently on the back cover blurb and were clearly trying so hard not to giggle out loud that they looked like their heads were about to pop. Then, after another minute or two, that same boy whose name I will never know crouched low, sprang upward like a frog and slam-dunked the DVD back into its position on the top shelf.

I frowned and turned away. But only for a second. The same darting movement caused me to turn again. This time, it was Jay who jumped. I saw him bend his knees, spring upward with all the force he could muster and topple a DVD with his outstretched fingertips from the top shelf.

Again, the boys huddled together to examine the information on the case and, again, whatever it was they saw almost caused them to have a hernia.

I looked upward in order to establish why exactly they were so fascinated with the films on the top shelf.

And then I realized.

I'm not going to go into any of the specifics but it's enough to say that those films on the top shelf were grubby.

Before I could stop myself, I said, 'Urrggghhhh! Yuck!' And then I shook my head in disgust at the two Year 9 boys and said, 'Virgins!' I said it very quietly though because I'm not stupid. I've got myself into trouble before for saying things like this.

Even though they have bad teeth, there obviously wasn't anything wrong with their ears. The nameless boy shoved the grubby film behind his back and, in a blatantly unfriendly manner, said, 'Did you just say something to me?'

'I doubt it,' I said and glared at him, even though I was actually feeling quite scared.

'Yeah, well . . . you better not have done,' he said, glaring back at me.

'Well, I didn't,' I said, still glaring.

The nameless boy shrugged and then he nodded in my

direction and said, 'Lesbian!' And then him and the boy called Jay both started laughing their heads off.

I hurriedly slammed *Forrest Gump* back on the shelf and walked straight out of the shop. Once outside, I rushed as fast as I could through the rain, and I didn't actually care which direction I was moving in – I just wanted to put some serious distance between myself and those stupid boys. And it wasn't what they'd *said* which bothered me exactly. It was more the fact that I was all on my own and I didn't have Gareth beside me to go all red in the face and tell them to apologize or Goose to tell them that they were being totally and utterly ridiculously ridonkulous.

But she *had* said it when we were barely three quarters of an hour outside Cardiff and speeding westward along the motorway to Aberystwyth. We'd spread ourselves out across the entire back seat of the coach. Left to right – Goose then Gareth then me. To begin with, as the bus station disappeared behind us, we'd all been a bit quiet. But then, at pretty much the exact same moment that it properly dawned on me that the coach *was* moving and we *were* on it, Gareth had said, 'Flipping heck! I can't believe this is actually happening! Flipping flopping flumping heck!'

And I said, 'This must be the most freakily freaked-out experience in the whole of Freaky-Experience Land.'

And Goose said, 'Yeah, and we're going to miss school tomorrow.'

For some reason, even though we all quite like school, that made us start to laugh. Not proper outright ha ha ha belly laughter, but just a light display of vocal amusement shared between three friends.

And then, with no warning whatsoever, Gareth narrowed his eyes, curled his top lip into a sneer, and in the dodgiest American accent that I've ever heard in my entire life, said, 'Don't be a spanner – Go to Pontcanna!'

'Huh?' I said.

'What?' said Goose.

Gareth grinned. 'Sorry, girls, it's a reflex. I just saw the name Pontcanna on a signpost and I couldn't stop myself. It's a game me and the rugby boys play when we're on the tour bus. What we do is, we spot a place name and we make up some rhyme to go with it. And the first line has to begin with the word *Don't* and the second line has to begin with the word *Go*. I don't know why – it's just the rules. Helps pass the time though and works a treat at breaking up any pre-match tension. Even Coach Jenkins sometimes joins in. Oh, and the really tricky part is that you gotta try and sound like Al Pacino in *The Godfather* when you say it.'

'I don't know who that is,' I said. 'I don't watch old films. Except *Star Wars*.'

'I've seen it,' said Goose. 'It's a classic. Tim booked it for the Sunday film club the other week. Tim reckons that it's widely regarded to be the second greatest film in the whole of American cinematic history.' Her face darkened a bit then and she said, 'I should be with Tim right now. I think I'm probably going to get sacked.'

Me and Gareth exchanged a worried look. I'm hopeless in awkward situations, I really am. Luckily though, Gareth is a social genius. He glanced past Goose at the city flashing by on the other side of the window and then pointed a finger straight in her face and said, 'Don't act like a clown – Go to Grangetown!'

'Gareth, that game is hilarious,' said Goose flatly and mouthed the word *sad* at me. But a split second after that, she glanced out of the window, turned back to us with her eyes half-closed and her jaw jutting forward aggressively and said, 'Don't do things by half – go to Penarth!'

And even though her Al Pacino impression was as rubbish as an empty Ribena carton, and even though this was without any shadow of a doubt the worst and most tragic game ever invented in the entire history of tragic games, we all burst out laughing. And this time it was actual ha ha ha belly laughter rather than the light vocal display of amusement that it had been earlier. But the really weird thing was that once we'd started to laugh, we couldn't stop. We physically couldn't. Because no sooner would we be getting to the end of our ha has, than one or other of us would hold an imaginary cigar in our hand and say something like, 'Don't follow the trend – go to Bridgend!' And that would set us off again. Like this:

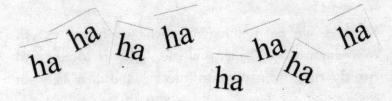

When you really think about it, it wasn't even *that* funny. In fact, it wasn't funny at all. Actually, to be brutally honest, it put the un in funny. And yet at the same time, it was flipping flopping flumping hysterical.

But then, one by one, once we'd all got totally stuck trying to think of something that would rhyme with either

Ystradgynlais or Pontneddfechan, the ha has dried up and we went a bit quiet. And then we pretty much went silent.

And, somehow, the atmosphere changed. I don't know why. The bus was the same. The situation was the same. But our faces underwent a catastrophic transformation. We looked like this:

For ages, we said nothing and then, just before we got to Swansea, Goose sighed and said, 'This is totally and utterly ridiculously ridonkulous!' And then she went silent again.

I wriggled uneasily in my seat. 'I didn't make you come with me,' I said.

Goose leaned forward to look at me. And it was that exact same kind of look that teachers give you when they'd really like to clip you round the ear but know they're not allowed to. Like this:

'Oh jog on,' said Goose crossly. 'I was hardly going to leave you standing at the bus stop, was I?'

'Well you could've done,' I said, hurt. 'I only asked to lend some money.'

'Borrow!' said Goose.

'OK, borrow then. Keep your baggy bra on.'

Gareth, who'd been sitting very quietly between the two of us, raised his palms into the air and said, 'Ladies, please! We're on a public bus and we're representing Cardiff here! Can we try and show a bit of decorum?'

'Huh?' I said.

'What?' said Goose.

Gareth's cheeks reddened. 'Well, it's the kind of thing Coach Jenkins says when it gets a bit rowdy on the rugby coach and it usually works for him. But, honestly, don't start rowing, eh? I'm getting a dose of the Frillies. And I really, really don't need it right now.' His cheeks went redder. For one weird horrible second, I glimpsed a glassiness in his eyes and actually thought he might be about to cry. But it must have just been a bit of dust which had irritated him or something, because he fiddled with his eyelashes for a moment, then blew his cheeks out in a big noisy sigh and said, 'Right! To action. Goose, can you borrow me your phone for a second? I gotta make a really important call to Coach Jenkins. Tell him where I am.' And then, miserably and almost to himself, he mumbled, 'He's gonna totally kill me.'

For a moment, Goose looked like she was on the verge of saying something critical to Gareth but whatever it was she obviously decided against it. Biting her lip quite blatantly, she said, 'Sure.' Then she rummaged in her briefcase, pulled out her phone and added, 'And after he's finished, you have to phone your mum, Lottie, and tell her where you are. That was part of the deal, remember?'

I nodded. I didn't mind. In actual fact, now that I was really and properly on my way to Aberystwyth, I *wanted* to phone my mum. I knew she'd be getting worried about me. If she'd noticed I'd gone, that is.

'Hello . . . Is that Coach Jenkins?' Gareth had Goose's phone pressed flat against his right ear and his hand pressed flat against his left ear. 'Hello — it's Gareth, it is. . . . Yeah, I know, that's why I'm phoning. I'm sorry, Coach, I . . . What's that? I can't hear you properly. . . . Hello? . . . Hello? . . . Coach? . . . Are you there?'

Evidently, despite the fact that Gareth was booming so loud that everyone on our coach definitely *could* hear him, the only Coach that mattered obviously *couldn't*. Gareth lowered his arm and stared down at the phone with a look of total dismay on his face.

'No signal?' I asked anxiously.

'No credit?' Goose asked, sounding equally anxious. 'Because it's OK – I've got a top-up card in my bag somewhere.'

Gareth shook his head. 'No, that won't help! Cos there's no flipping charge!' A look of horror had spread over his face. 'Your battery is totally and utterly kaput, Goose. Dead as a doughnut. So a great flipping flat use of good this is!' And then he pushed the phone back into Goose's hands, folded his arms and slumped so far down in his seat that I thought he was going to slip right off the edge and collapse on to the floor.

Goose's face clouded. 'I don't believe it,' she said. 'The number of times I've said that my battery is flat! And it's always been a total lie to get me out of a boring conversation. And now my battery actually is flat and I really really need my stupid phone.'

'How am I going to phone my mum?' I asked.

'Well, you're not, are you?' said Gareth, a lot more crossly than he needed. 'Not just now, anyway. Same as I ain't gonna speak to Coach Jenkins and tell him where the heck I am.'

My mum has always said to me that if I'm ever in a situation where I can't think of anything good to say, I should say nothing.

So I said nothing and looked out of the window. Outside, towering above all the terraced houses and telegraph poles, I spotted the Liberty Stadium, home of Swansea's football and rugby teams. I'd seen it on the telly loads of times but I'd never actually seen it with my own personal actual eyes before. Hoping to improve Gareth's mood a little, I nudged him in the side and said, 'I can see the Liberty Stadium over there, Gaz.'

Gareth's frown deepened and he made no effort to look in the direction I was indicating. 'I'm a Cardiff Blues man myself,' he said. 'I hate the Ospreys. They represent everything in life that I object to.' And then he unzipped his bag, pulled out his iPod, plugged his earphones into his lugholes and shut his eyes. Conversation blatantly over.

Goose, who now had her feet up on the seat and was leaning with her back to the window, put her head on one side so that she could see beyond Gareth to talk to me. 'Look,' she said, 'I'm sorry I got so stroppy just now. I just got a bit stressed out. This is a helluva situation we're in. But your sister will have a phone, won't she? She'll let us all borrow it, won't she?'

'Course she will,' I said. 'She's as sound as a pound that got found on the ground is my sister Ruthie. Honestly she is.'

because of some kind of gravity problem I have. No matter how hard I try to fight against it, whenever I'm walking up a hill or down a hill, I end up waving my arms and legs around and generally walking like one of those weird wooden Thunderbird puppets that are sometimes on TV during the school holidays – and that's not really an image I'm chasing. Also, as far as I could tell, it's impossible to walk anywhere in Aberystwyth for more than a few seconds at a time without running into a big group of students who aren't looking where they're going and barge you off the pavement. And then, too, there was the fact that we didn't have a map. I had to ask several people the way to Ruthie's street and I think the first person I spoke to sent us wandering off in the wrong direction just for the hell of it. Only Gareth seemed confident about finding his way around because he'd visited the town a few times to play rugby. But that didn't mean he was any help. He kept saying stuff like, 'Oh I remember where I am now. Definitely. Just round this next corner, there's this legendary little boozer where we all went out and got totally battered after beating Penweddig School 34–0 . . .' And then we'd walk around the corner and there'd just be a church or a Scout hut.

Eventually, though, after walking like a Thunderbird puppet for about thirty minutes, I came to a halt at the address that I know off by heart and which happens to be where my sister lives. Goose and Gareth came to a halt too. We were standing in front of a big grey house that looked as if it was made out of concrete and had lots of different-sized dirty windows. Someone had sprayed some fake snow in the corners of the windows but this only made the house look even more tragic. I don't mean to be rude but I think it was very possibly the ugliest house I've ever seen. Loud music could be heard playing inside even though all the odd-sized windows were closed.

'Is this it then?' said Gareth, running his hands over his rugby top in what I guessed was a fairly pointless attempt to make himself look smarter. 'Doesn't look much of a place, does it?'

'It'll be all right inside,' said Goose brightly. 'Ring the bell, Lottie. It's freezing out here.'

I pushed the buzzer.

No one came.

I pushed the buzzer again.

Still no one came.

'This is definitely the right address,' I said. 'Maybe she can't hear us because of all that crappy music.'

'Try knocking,' said Gareth, and then he leaned over my shoulder and hammered on the door himself.

'Easy, Gaz,' I said. 'You don't wanna break the door down!'

Inside, the music stopped. We heard some laughter and voices and then the sound of feet in noisy heels running down uncarpeted stairs.

'Must be one of her mates,' I said knowingly to the other two. 'Ruthie doesn't wear girly heels. She's an archaeology student.'

But, then, as plain as a poppadom, I heard Ruthie's voice. 'You're too early,' she shouted from behind the heavy wooden front door. 'The party hasn't even started yet!' The door opened inward and my sister's face peered around it.

'What the—' she said, and then stopped abruptly and gazed at me in amazement.

It wasn't *pleased*-looking amazement.

I gazed back at her. It was my sister and yet it *wasn't* my sister. Not a version of her that I'm familiar with anyway. She was wearing a silky black top with spaghetti straps, skinny jeans and a pair of very pointy, *very* high heeled shoes. Evidently, she'd recently stepped out of the bathroom because her hair was all hidden in a carefully twisted towel. In one hand, she was holding a large glass of red wine.

'Lottie, what are you doing here?' she said. 'And why have you got grey hair?'

I bit my lip nervously and, with a small shrug, I said, 'I don't know.' And those three little words were probably among the truest that I've ever spoken.

a NOt PartICuLarLY GreY weDNesDaY MOrNING IN wreXham

I'm back in Wrexham library. I like it here. It's a good place to sit in peace and think and type. Last night, I didn't get a spare second to myself because I was babysitting Caradoc while my dad took Sally Frizz out for a drink. I don't mind though because Caradoc is cute and I don't get to see him all that often. We played a made-up game called Kill Darth Vader. I was Darth Vader and Caradoc was Luke Skywalker and I had to hide somewhere in the house and breathe really noisily like I had a serious lung disease and then Caradoc would come and find me and kill me with his plastic lightsabre. It was quite an enjoyable game actually but three hours of it was probably too much.

Then, this morning, after Sally had returned from taking Caradoc to school, she said, 'You can't monopolize that computer all day again today, Lottie. I need it to see if I've had any new orders.'

'I know,' I said. 'I didn't monopolize it yesterday either. I went into town, remember.'

But I don't think that Sally heard me properly because she said, 'That's a great idea! Why don't you go and have another look around today.'

It wasn't a question. I don't even think it was a suggestion.

'OK,' I said. 'I haven't got any money though.'

This wasn't strictly true. I still had seven pounds left over from yesterday. I'd only bought myself a can of Coke and a sandwich all day. I didn't see why Sally should be able to throw me out of the house free of charge though.

'Five pounds,' said Sally, taking a note out of her purse, 'that's all I can afford to give you. And make it last, please. I mean . . . you may find that you want to go into town tomorrow as well.'

'Oh no,' I said. 'I think I'd prefer to just stay indoors tomorrow. I'm sure I'll have been around all the shops pretty thoroughly by the end of today.'

Sally didn't say anything but just gave me a tight-lipped smile and for a second I wondered if I'd said something wrong. But then she glanced out of the window and said, 'That stupid man at number fifteen is parking too close to my Micra again,' and went rushing off outside to moan at him before he disappeared. To be honest, I think Sally is simply one of those people who exist in a permanent state of panic.

So I walked into town again. The sky was the same dark grey colour as yesterday. Nobody else seemed bothered by it though. It was also raining again, but this time, instead of the fat heavy raindrops of yesterday, it was an annoying blanket of drizzle, which got in my face and made my hair turn into frizz. Maybe it's the rain that has ruined Sally's hair? Pulling up the hood of Ruthie's parka, I headed straight for one of the big indoor market halls.

Wrexham has got three of them. The one I went to first

and the one I like the best is called the Butchers' Market. The reason I like it is because it's just like the market hall in the centre of Cardiff. In fact, it's so similar that once I was inside I was even able to pretend that Goose and Gareth and my house and my school were just a short bus ride away on the other side of the thick brick walls.

There are a lot of interesting things to look at in that market. Despite being called the Butchers' Market, it sells absolutely everything – not just hunks of raw meat. In one corner there was a magician who was pulling coins from out of the ears of anyone daft enough to pause for more than half a second in front of his stall. Personally, I don't like magic tricks or magicians because they give me the shuddery spooks so I hurried past him and made a point of not looking anywhere in his general direction. Another stall sold nothing but brightly coloured covers to snap over your mobile phone. I stood for quite a long while in front of that one. For ages, I was torn between buying myself a phone cover decorated with rabbits or one with Jimi Hendrix's face on it but, just as I was about to get my purse out of my pocket, I remembered that I'd left my phone in Cardiff and I couldn't be bothered to buy either of them after that.

And then I felt a bit sad for a while. I really miss my phone. I miss it even more than my hair-straighteners and that's saying something because – as well as being grey – my hair at the moment looks not entirely dissimilar to this:

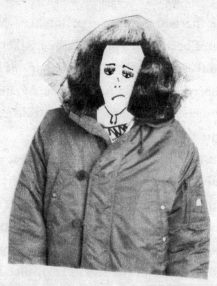

Looks-wise, it's fair to say that I'm not at my personal best. Currently, because of my lack of hair-straighteners, it's very difficult to spot the difference between my hair and my synthetic furry hood. But if I was offered the choice of being reunited with my hair-straighteners or my phone, I'd still rather have my phone. As luck would have it, I'm not actually being offered either.

The thing I really miss is having constant text access to Gareth and Goose because I haven't heard from either of them since my dad came and collected me from Aberystwyth and I desperately need to talk to them about what happened in the kitchen at Ruthie's party. Even more than that, I miss being able to speak to my mum whenever I want. I did speak to her briefly on my dad's phone last night but it was highly awkward. All the time I was talking, Caradoc wouldn't leave me alone and kept asking me to play Kill Darth Vader with him. I found it very hard to say all the things that I needed to.

My mum is very upset with me.

It's not something that I wish to deal with right now — here in a public place — so I'm going to return to my description of the Butchers' Market.

In the Butchers' Market, there's also a stall that sells pet products and I hung around it for ages because I love the smell of pet shops. Although it's probably not to everybody's taste, I love the furry fustiness and general aroma of pet-food pellets and sawdust. I think it's a very comforting smell. Unfortunately, it also reminded me of Winnie, my elderly pet chinchilla, who I've thoughtlessly abandoned in Cardiff. This made me feel sad all over again and I spent 75 pence of my money on some forest fruit-flavoured yoghurt drops for him. I'm not sure when he'll actually get to eat them though.

After that, I found a stall called . . .

T-shirtz 4 All Occasionz

. . . which makes total perfect sense because they actually *do* have every type of T-shirt imaginable. But just in case, they also have a **While-U-W8** printing service. I flicked my finger along all the hanging rails and found a T-shirt that I knew at once would make a really good Christmas present for Gareth.

The stallholder was a big man with big sideburns and a smiley face. He reminded me of Elvis Presley a little bit. When I held out the T-shirt to him and asked if I could buy it, he said, 'Are you sure you want just the one shirt, love? It's Wonder Bargain Wednesday today. One shirt for a fiver or two for eight quid. You won't find a better deal than that in the whole of Wales. Tempted?'

'Yes,' I said, because I love a bargain.

I went back to the rails again and had another good rummage but this time I couldn't find anything that properly floated my boat and flipped my ship so I went back to the man to pay for my one T-shirt and then I suddenly had an idea.

'Does the Wonder Bargain Wednesday offer still apply if I have a T-shirt printed exclusively for me?'

The smiley man with the sideburns said, 'Not usually, my

darling. But seeing as it's for you and I'm not particularly rushed off my feet, I don't see why I can't make an exception just this once.' And then he handed me a T-shirt-shaped piece of paper and a pencil so that I could draw my own design. When I'd finished, I handed the paper and pencil back to him. It was a serious Type A fashion statement. The smiley man stuck the pencil behind his ear, looked at what I'd written and grinned.

'It's just something that cheers me up,' I said. I think my cheeks had gone a bit red. They certainly felt quite hot.

Smiley sideburn man grinned again. 'I'm not knocking it, love; I like it. I think I'll have one of these printed for myself as well. Anyway, it'll be ready in a couple of hours. OK?'

'OK,' I said and shrugged. I wasn't in any hurry anyway. Sally had told me that four o'clock would be the most convenient time for me to return to the house.

So I went and sat in a little cafe which was tucked alongside one wall of the market and which was called The Good Friends Cafe. It had pea-green bathroom tiles on the walls and white plastic tables covered in red and white chequered tablecloths. On the tables were squeezy ketchup bottles in the shape of giant plastic tomatoes. This really cheered me up because anyone with half a head knows that ketchup always tastes better when it comes from a giant plastic tomato. Apart from me, all the other people who were sitting in there looked like they were at least seventy years old. I took Ruthie's coat off and sat down. A large lady who had been peeling potatoes behind a counter waddled over to me and said, 'What you having?' Considering that it was called The Good Friends Cafe, she wasn't very friendly. In fact, someone – but not me – should tell her to go and have a good long chat with the smiley sideburn man from the T-shirt stall because he's very friendly and could teach her a few customer service skills.

I couldn't see any menus anywhere so I just asked for my favourite drink. 'Um, I'll have a double choco-mochaccino with extra cream and marshmallows, please.'

'No you won't,' said the unfriendly woman.

'Oh,' I said.

'You can have tea or coffee. Or at a push, I can make you a Horlicks.'

'Oh,' I said again. I didn't know what a Horlicks was. I still don't. 'Can I have a coffee then, please?' I said.

'Black or white?'

'White,' I said.

'Instant or frothy?'

'Er . . . frothy.' I wasn't totally sure what she was on about. We don't have this sort of coffee in Cardiff. In Cardiff, it's a lot more straightforward – we only have lattes, cappuccinos, skinny lattes, skinny cappuccinos and double choco-mochaccinos. With extra cream and marshmallows, if desired.

'Sugar, saccharin or nothing?'

'Er . . . nothing,' I said. I didn't know what saccharin was. I still don't. And I could see the sugar bowl from where I was sitting. It was on the counter and it wasn't a bowl so much as it was a tub. A discoloured yellowing tub with the faded word SUGAR taped on to the lid. I could feel myself losing weight just by looking at it.

But when my un-sugared frothy coffee arrived, it was actually really nice. I sipped it ever so slowly so that it would last for ages and while I sat there, I watched the people of Wrexham as they rushed around the market doing their shopping. And when I got bored of doing that I had a good look around The Good Friends Cafe, and pinned on to the wall I saw some words that were printed on a tea towel and said this:

'There are big ships and small ships but the best ship of all is FRIENDSHIP'
— Author Unknown

The unfriendly large lady had put down her potato peeler and was now wiping some tables with a damp cloth. She moved over to where I was sitting and swooshed her cloth over my table – which still had somebody else's stray baked bean on it. 'I see you're looking at those words of wisdom over there,' she said to me.

'Mmm,' I said. I didn't really want to talk to her but I was too frightened not to answer. And anyway, that would have been totally rude.

'Don't believe a single blinking word of it,' she said, nodding her head at the tea towel. 'If your life turns out to be half as fascinating as mine, you'll soon see that there aren't any big ships *or* small ships. Just nothin' but hardships and a whole string of useless bloody relationships.'

And then she sniffed and waddled off to wipe the next table. I frowned and stared down at the surface of my table. The stray baked bean was now gone but had been replaced instead by a small pool of water with a single long hair floating in the middle of it.

I finished my frothy coffee quickly after that. Leaving The Good Friends Cafe, I went to the loo in the market hall, sat under the hand dryer for a while to get myself warmed up and then had another wander around the shopping streets of Wrexham. It's not like Cardiff. It doesn't even have a *small* branch of Maxi Style – let alone the four floors of fashion at cost-cutting prices that we have in Cardiff. Somehow, though, I managed to waste an hour and a quarter and then I went back to see the man on the T-shirt stall.

He looked at his watch and said, 'You're an early bird.'

'I know, I always catch the worm,' I said. I was just making small talk to be honest. But also I wanted to check that my voice still worked. I hadn't used it for ages.

'Well, you're lucky I'm so organized. Your T-shirt

looks cracking,' he said and handed it to me in a stripy red polythene bag. 'Have a good rest of the day now, kiddo. Doing anything nice?'

'I doubt it,' I said. 'But thanks for asking.'

And then I took the stripy bag, tucked it inside the one with Gareth's T-shirt in, and wandered slowly over here to the library. And this is where I'm going to stay until it's almost four o'clock and safe to go back to the house.

what haPPeNeD IN the kItCheN
at the PartY[23]

'And this . . .' said my sister Ruthie, waving her finger around the kitchen, '. . . is where you're all going to stay until the party's over.'

'In the kitchen?' said Gareth. 'All night?'

Ruthie glared at him. 'I mean it! The three of you are to stay in here where I can keep an eye on you.' Then she looked straight at me and said, 'Seriously, Lottie, you've put me in a really impossible position. Your timing is un-flipping-believable!'

'It's a Sunday,' I said. 'What kind of maniac has a party on a Sunday?'

Ruthie just shook her head at me in amazement. 'Oh, get with it, sis. Sunday is the new Saturday. I thought anyone with a slice of style knew that.' Then she looked all annoyed again and added, 'And me and my housemates have been planning this party for weeks and now you've rocked up with your kiddy-mates and none of you are *even* sixteen! What the heck will Mum say if anything bad happens? In the eyes of the law, I'm responsible for all of you. I'm your legal guardian!'

I rolled my eyes and said, 'Oh jog on!' I said it really quietly though because Ruthie was looking well dangerous.

---

[23] This is likely to be a long chapter because a lot happened.

'What did you just say to me?' demanded Ruthie.

'Ladies,' said Gareth, and raised his hands palm up in a peacekeeping gesture, 'We're in Aberystwyth and we should try to remember that we're all representing Cardiff here! Can we try and show a bit of decorum?'

Ruthie stopped glaring at me and glared at Gareth. 'What?'

Gareth grinned sheepishly and, even though I was in the middle of an extremely tense situation, that sheepish grin was so cute and so lovely that it made me want to grin too and so I did.

Ruthie must have eyes in the back of her head because she spotted it. 'This isn't funny, Lottie!' she said, staring at me again. 'You've run away from home and you've dragged your two chums along with you. Have you got any idea how utterly selfish that is?'

I felt uncomfortable then and the grin slipped off my face. I couldn't think of a good response so I just said, 'Keep your wig on.'

'Look,' said Gareth, laying his arms across mine and Goose's shoulders, 'these two won't get into any mischief, I promise you. I'm *personally* looking after them.'

Even Goose must have thought that was cute. Surely.

Gareth continued, 'But to be fair, it's bound to get a bit lively in this kitchen. I mean . . . look at all the booze you've got in here!'

He had a point. The work surfaces were piled so high with bottles and cans that the whole place looked more like a very scruffy off-licence than any kind of kitchen. I looked round a bit more. There was stuff everywhere. And it was all random scatty stuff. Like empty pizza boxes on the floor and photos of people's faces in close-up on the walls and a couple of For Sale boards shoved into one corner and a complete set of Take That dolls on the window ledge. Obviously, somebody in the house blatantly didn't like Gary Barlow because I could see that his head had a drawing pin in it and was connected to his body with sticky tape. Pinned by a magnet to the door of the fridge was a shopping list that said:

Shopping List

Cheap pasta
Cheap cheese
bread
milk
32 x cans of lager

My mum would've had a fit if she'd seen it.

And the entire kitchen stank of stale beer and cigarettes and mashed potato.

Embarrassed, I glanced back at Goose and Gareth and saw that Gareth was staring up at the ceiling. He'd gone very red in the face. I looked up too. Above our heads was a massive poster of Britney Spears wearing nothing but a skimpy gold bra and skimpy gold hot pants. I'd seen this poster before – it's actually the exact same one that Gareth has got stuck to the ceiling above his bed. But the one crucial difference between Gareth's poster and the one in my sister's manky kitchen was that someone had replaced Britney's head with a big photo of Ruthie's.

Gareth cleared his throat. And then he said to Ruthie, 'Perhaps it would be better if we just stayed in your bedroom and kept ourselves to ourselves.'

'No way!' Ruthie looked genuinely alarmed. 'I'm not leaving you tucked up in my bedroom with my little sister. Mum would kill me. And anyway, it wouldn't be fair on Goose.'

Gareth looked confused. Goose just mumbled, 'Oh, don't mind me. Nobody else ever does.' She looked fed up. I'm not surprised though. She was still wearing that hideous blue and yellow uniform.

'No,' said Ruthie. 'You all stay in here and you do not leave this kitchen until I say. And then you . . .' she pointed her finger at Gareth, '. . . are sleeping down here on the couch and you two can squeeze into my double bed with me.' And then she looked up at the Britney Biggs poster and made a big angry frustrated noise which went like this:

Oooooooffffff

When she was all oooooofffed out, she pulled a mobile phone out of her pocket and said, 'But right now, Lottie, you're going to ring Mum and tell her where you are.'

I panicked. 'She'll kill me.'

'Good. I'll help her,' said Ruthie.

'Please, Ruthie . . .' I begged. 'I can't. It's so difficult. She expects me to play happy families with her new boyfriend and his weird emo daughter and I just can't cope with it.'

Ruthie's eyebrows nearly flew off her head. 'What? Mum's got a new boyfriend?'

She was blatantly gobsmacked. 'Whoops,' I said.

Ruthie went quiet and stared at me for a very long moment. Then she said, '*I'll* phone her and tell her where you are—'

'I'm not going back,' I said.

'I'll phone her,' said Ruthie, ignoring me, '. . . and then you two . . .' she said, looking at Goose and Gareth, '. . . can call your parents as well. Agreed?'

Goose and Gareth nodded quickly.

Ruthie walked to the kitchen door, 'Oh, and if I find out that ANY ONE OF YOU so much as sniffs ANY of this alcohol at ANY point during this evening, I will PERSONALLY see to it that your lives are ruined FOREVER. AND I SERIOUSLY MEAN THAT.'

Then she disappeared through the doorway and up to her room so that she could go and make that terrible phone call without all of us listening.

'Well, that went well,' said Goose. 'Do you think that now would be a good time to ask her if I can borrow some party clothes?'

I looked at Goose. 'Er . . . I don't think so.'

Goose rolled her eyes and said, 'Actually, darling, I was being facetious.'

Goose is very good with words. I am too but Goose is better.

Gareth, who has colossal manly thighs but doesn't have such a good way with words, just said, 'You two are doing my flipping flopping flumping head in,' and then he started hunting for the kettle so that he could make us all a cup of coffee.

It wasn't the last cup of coffee we had that evening. Ruthie's party lasted until

. . . or, at least, that was the time on Ruthie's digital clock just before I got to squeeze into her over-occupied bed and finally – thankfully – made the world disappear for a while.

And that left the three of us with a lot of time to drink coffee. And chat. And to witness with our own eyes the totally freakish behaviour of my sister's friends as they let their scruffy student hair down. Ruthie has more friends than I ever could have imagined. And judging by all the

Double Denim[24] on display, a good percentage of them most definitely fall into the Type C category for colossal fashion failures. We could see loads of them through the doorway of the kitchen, squashed together in the hall like denim-wearing sardines. Some of them were dad-dancing to an ancient hip hop record that was being played so loudly that it felt like all the walls were p-u-l-s-a-t-i-n-g and others were standing one millimetre apart and having shouted conversations into each other's faces. And every few seconds, the crush of people hanging around the door would be pushed apart as someone barged into our stinking kitchen to get more beer. To begin with, I tried to be friendly to Ruthie's mates but then a girl in a Double Denim miniskirt and bra combination started hanging around and sticking her chest out at Gareth and this made me a lot less friendly. Fortunately, I don't think Gareth was at all fussed by her or her chest because he was too busy building an Eiffel Tower out of cardboard beer mats and didn't even bother to stop what he was doing and check her out.

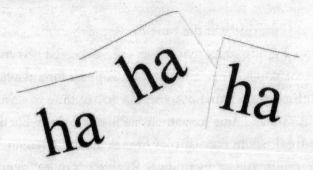

---

[24] Jeans are cool. Denim jackets are cool. BUT NOT TOGETHER.

After that, Goose and I started pretending that we were called Olga and Inga and that we came from Moscow – just so that we didn't have to talk to anyone else. And then Gareth joined in and pretended that he was called Boris from St Petersburg. I think me and Goose actually fooled a lot of people because we had really wicked Russian accents but I don't think anyone believed Gareth because he sounded like a Mexican. And anyway, he was still wearing his Wales rugby kit.

But at some point during that weird evening, we also found the time to go mad.

And I mean completely moon howling mad.

Now, I'll be honest – *I* have a bit of a history of this kind of thing. I know I have. I'm not going to deny it. I've been seeing a counsellor called Blake and he's been helping me to develop strategies to manage my madder moments. And, on the whole, I've been coping pretty well, I think. But on Sunday night, in Ruthie's kitchen, I temporarily stopped coping and everything in my mind went totally wonk-side-up.

But what's double weird is that Goose and Gareth went even wonkier than I did and, as far as I'm aware, they're both a pair of utter normals. Especially Gareth.

So now that I find myself sitting in Wrexham library and raking over the nitty-gritties of that stressful evening, it seems only sensible to try to work out exactly what went wrong. And if this sounds like I'm dwelling on the past and crying over spilt milk and worrying about water that has already gone *way* under the bridge, it's important to remember that sometimes you have to put your mind into reverse in order to make any positive progress. Or as some dead Danish bloke called Søren Kierkegaard once said:

Life can only be understood backwards; but it must be lived forwards.[25]

So I'm trying to understand it all backwards and I'm asking myself the following questions:

Did it all get so stressful because Ruthie had forgotten to feed us and we were slowly starving to death?

Or was it the fact that approximately two hundred students were jam-packed into a modestly sized terraced house and were replacing all the vital oxygen supplies with powerful clouds of nerd gas?

Or was it simply that Goose and Gareth have one or two mental problems of their own?

Maybe.

Or maybe it was all just the fault of Ruthie's boyfriend, Michel. Because we'd been OK until he rocked up. We'd each drunk about eight cups of coffee and were doing some

---

[25] I haven't spent ALL of my time in this library just typing up my stream of consciousness and staring at a laminated poster on the wall opposite called 'Small Mammals of Great Britain'. I've also been looking at some books about philosophy. Allow me to introduce Søren Kierkegaard – born in Copenhagen in 1813. He said a lot of VERY INTELLIGENT THINGS. Most of them I don't understand.

deliberate dad-dancing in the stinking kitchen. And at the same time, we were pretending to be Russian and playing the Place Name game, using any city in the world that we could think of. Me and Goose were really good at it because we're women and we can naturally multitask but Gareth was struggling to think *and* be Russian *and* move his feet at the same time. I was tickling him with Gary Barlow's feet, which probably didn't help. And Goose had moved on from dad-dancing and was trying instead to break-dance on her head. In short, we were having a laugh. And then Michel barged his way in.

Michel is French. Just like Ruthie, he's an archaeology student. He's quite good-looking and has lovely long eyelashes but his trousers are always far too short so that his mustard-coloured socks are permanently on display. Despite knowing nothing about trousers, Michel is actually very knowledgeable in many other areas and always has a great deal to say. Unfortunately, none of it is interesting.

I spotted Michel's face emerge from the dark hallway at the exact same moment that Goose was performing a handstand and yelling, 'Don't be embarrassed – Go to Paris!'

Michel stood blinking for a moment in the bright light of the kitchen and then he frowned at her. Suddenly spotting me on the other side of the kitchen, he smiled widely and shouted, 'Dottie!'

'It's actually *Lottie*,' I shouted back. Even though the music was coming from other parts of the house, it was still pretty noisy in our kitchen. And added to this was the noise of the neighbours who kept thumping on the walls and not in time with the music. I noticed a cork from a wine bottle lying on the floor and wondered if it would be any good as a makeshift ear-defender. I stooped down, picked it up and contemplated shoving it in my ear but then decided it was a stupid idea and shoved it into my pocket instead.

'Dottie,' said Michel and, grabbing me by the shoulders, he kissed me on both cheeks. 'Ruthie was saying that you was here in the party but I was not believing her.' And then he looked at Goose who had just crashed back to her feet and said, 'But, in reality, how can it possibly be embarrassing to go to Paris? Paris is beautiful, no? Paris is—'

'No, no . . . It's just a game,' said Goose quickly.

But Michel said, 'Yes, in fact, Paris is certainly one of the most beautiful and romantic cities in the world. And it has been an important human habitation for more than two millions of years. How can this be an embarrassing situation? It has grown up from being a tiny island community on the Seine river to becoming one of the greatest urban populations on Earth. It is an important centre for arts and culture and history but also, in reality, for the entire global economy. In fact, it is the sixth most important economic centre in the entire world and the most important one in the entire space of Europe. Even more so than your capital city of London. And Paris—'

'Mate, I'm Welsh,' boomed Gareth firmly. 'Cardiff is *my* capital.'

But Michel just said, '– has plenty plenty of millions of tourists who visit and take home happy souvenirs every single year. And plenty plenty of these tourists return to take more happy souvenirs in the following years. In reality, it is one of the most popular tourist destinations in the entire world. It has plenty plenty attractions to see and marvellous architectures and galleries of art and beautiful gardens . . . And you think this is a reason to feel embarrassing?'

'Someone please help me,' said Goose.

I spotted another stray cork on the floor and put that into my pocket too.

Michel said, 'Yes, but Paris is—'

Gareth said, 'Mate, do you wanna cup of coffee?'

Michel looked confused for a second. Then he looked at all the bottles and cans that were stacked on the work surfaces and said, 'But no, I prefer to take a glass of wine.'

All three of us gave a visible and blatant sigh of relief. At least he'd shut up about Paris. Gareth passed Michel a plastic cup and then boiled the kettle and made us three more cups of coffee.

Michel had moved over to the bottle-covered worktop and was studying the labels on various bottles of wine, a look of disappointment growing on his face. Finally, shaking his head, he said, 'In reality, the attitude of the English is—'

'We're Welsh,' shouted me, Goose and Gareth.

Michel just said, 'In reality, the attitude of the Welsh is very naive for the purchase of the wines. In France, we look to see what kind of grapes has been used in the manufacturing process and also where the wine has been produced and bottled but, in the actual fact, here in England, it—'

'Wales!'

'– here in Wales, it is simply the level of the alcoholic content and the cheap price which is the primary concerns and this is a great pity because much pleasurable experience is lost in the drinking. No? But, in any case, the wine here is—'

'Mate,' said Gareth holding up his hand. 'Stop! Please! You're boring my pants off.'

Goose looked at Gareth and started to giggle.

Michel looked confused and then he looked a bit hurt.

I'll be honest, I was a bit startled by Gareth's outburst. Gareth is usually the most patient human person I've ever encountered. I frowned at him and said as quietly as I could, 'That was out of order, Gaz. Michel is my sister's boyfriend. He's practically family.'

Gareth downed his fresh coffee in one impossibly long gulp, put his mouth close to my ear and said, 'I don't care if he's Barack flipping flopping flumping Obama. He's still making my brain melt.'

And even though he was yelling, nobody other than me would have ever heard his words – had it not been for the fact that while he was speaking, the music abruptly stopped and everywhere was suddenly plunged into silence and darkness.

And then, outside the kitchen, the house erupted into a weird symphony of screams and cheers.

Inside the kitchen, I heard the unmistakable sound of Goose giggling even harder.

'Why have all the lights gone off?' I asked, adjusting my voice back to its normal volume.

Instead of answering me, Michel said, 'Yes, but apparently I am making your friend's pants fall down. This is a classic example of English anti-establishment behaviour. Here, in England, the young people have no sense of community or doing the social interactions with other society members and this is leading to—'

Gareth said, 'Oh, I'm sorry, Lottie. I can't cope with this. Anyway, I need to circulate. If I stay in here any longer, I'll go nuts. I'm going to find out what's happened.' Then he looked at Goose and said, 'Are you coming?'

'Huh?' I said. My jaw had fallen open.

Goose ignored me and shook her head. 'I'd love to, Gaz, but I'm wearing an usherette uniform.'

In the darkness, Gareth just shrugged and said, 'Who's gonna notice?' And then he said, 'Suit yourself,' and moved off towards the door.

'What?' I said. 'You can't go. Ruthie will kill me. And you.'

Gareth's dark shape said, 'I'll cross that bridge when I come to it,' and then he disappeared into the mass of screaming and cheering bodies in the hallway.

I turned back to the silhouette of Michel and said, 'Brilliant. Now look what you've done. You've bored my boyfriend out of the building.'

Michel said, 'Pfffff.' And then he said, 'Yes, but, in reality—'

'Oh pleeeease don't start going on about reality again,' wailed Goose.

'Hey,' I said, swinging around to face her. 'Back off and leave Michel alone. He's my sister's boyfriend.'

'All right,' said Goose. 'Keep your hairy tash on.'

'I haven't got a tash,' I said to Goose. And then I turned to Michel and demanded, 'Do you think I've got a tash?'

Michel said, 'No, I'm sorry, I don't understand. What is a tash?'

'A moustache,' I bellowed. I was starting to get very agitated. In my hands, I had a piece of cork that I'd picked up from somewhere and I was so stressed out that I snapped the thing completely in half and threw it at the wall. 'Do YOU think I've got a moustache?'

Michel looked even more confused and, after a moment's pause, he said, 'I cannot answer this question in the dark. I'm going to find out what has happened to the electricity.' Then he too disappeared into the crowded hallway.

Goose started laughing again. Even though I could barely see her, I could tell that she was borderline hysterical. 'He soooo thinks you've got a tash!'

'Shut up,' I said.

After a gulp of coffee, Goose said, 'No, I will not shut up! Get over yourself.'

For the second time in the space of minutes, my jaw fell open. 'Get over myself? What the heck is that supposed to mean?'

And then Goose did an extraordinary thing. She let go of her coffee mug and sent it crashing to the floor. Even in the dark, it looked pretty deliberate to me. I heard the sound of broken crockery smashing on the floor tiles.

'What did you do that for?' I said.

'Yeah,' said another voice that had arisen from nowhere and which I knew only too well. 'What did you do that for?'

It was Ruthie. She was holding a lighted candle in one hand and with her other she was dragging Gareth back into the kitchen by his ear. This wasn't easy because Gareth is about eight inches taller and three stones heavier than Ruthie. 'We forgot to feed the electricity meter,' she said before anyone had even asked. 'Michel's gone out to see if he can get some pound coins from the petrol station.' And then she said, 'Have you lot been drinking?'

'No,' we all said.

Ruthie took my mug from my hand and sniffed it suspiciously. 'Just coffee?'

'Yeah,' I said.

'So why are you throwing my mugs around? These things cost money, you know.'

'Sorry,' said Goose. And then she sighed noisily before adding, 'I dropped your mug and it smashed because there was nothing to save it – just like there's nothing out there to save any of us.'

Ruthie held her candle up towards Goose's face and peered at her. 'Are you sure you haven't been drinking?'

Goose nodded. 'I'm just having an existential crisis, that's all.'

Ruthie looked confused for a moment and then she said, 'Well, just be a bit more bloody careful with my cups.'

'Oh, chill out a bit, Ruthie,' I said. 'It was only a scatty old mug. And anyway, what's a few measly quid to you? You'd only waste it on booze.'

Ruthie glared at me. 'No I wouldn't.'

'Yeah you would,' I said. 'Because you're a student and that's all students *ever* spend their money on.'

'Er . . . excuse me,' said Ruthie, her face a spooky picture of candlelit outrage. 'I think you'll find that students spend their money on a lot of things.'

'Oh yeah,' chipped in Gareth, who was rubbing his ear and sounding cheesed off, 'Like what?'

'Like books . . .' said Ruthie.

'And?' This time it was Goose who wanted to know about the purchasing habits of the student population.

My sister held her candle up and glared at her. Then she

glared at all of us. And then she said, '. . . and paper and ink cartridges and food and the electricity meter . . .'

'Oh yeah,' said Gareth with a snort. 'I can really see that you spend *heaps* of money on that!'

'Er . . . excuse me, Gareth,' said my sister, '. . . remember whose sofa you're sleeping on tonight.'

Gareth sighed noisily. And then, because he must have had a death wish, he pointed at the dirty dishes in the minging sink and said, 'And cleaning products?'

'Yes . . . *and* cleaning products!' Ruthie was blatantly annoyed. She put her candle down and then, counting off each item on her fingers, she added, '. . . and library fines and archaeology field trips and tools for an archaeological dig . . . oh, and dwarf hats and mini pretend coal-miners' lanterns and . . .'

'Mini coal-miners' lanterns? Dwarf hats?' I can't remember who interrupted her. To be fair, it could have been any one of us.

'Yeah,' said Ruthie. 'Because we all went to a fancy-dress party dressed as Snow White and the Seven Dwarfs. Obviously!' And then she said, '. . . and fake beards and glow-sticks and takeaway chips and nightclub entrance fees and Do-it-Yourself mask kits and a 3D projector for our photos and Lego and shoes and funny fridge magnets and plastic cups and string and . . .'

This time it was definitely me who interrupted. 'Plastic cups and string?'

'Yeah,' said Ruthie. 'For making telephones. Obviously.'

'Oh yeah,' I said.

And then Ruthie said, '. . . and tubs of ice cream and board games and Chinese takeaways and kebabs and toasted-sandwich-making contraptions and charity-shop trinkets and second-hand cushion covers and energy drinks and . . . and . . .' Ruthie paused, and then she shook her head and said, 'No, I think that's pretty much everything.'

Goose said, 'Do you want me to pay for the mug?'

Ruthie muttered, 'Oh, forget it.' And then, after taking a box of candles from the cupboard under the sink, she disappeared back into the hallway.

The second she was gone, Gareth started opening cupboard doors. 'I'm starving. If I don't eat something soon, I'll collapse and die. And that's a fact.'

'You can't help yourself to her food,' I said.

'I can and I am,' said Gareth. And then, as if to demonstrate the fact, he waved a large bag of prawn cocktail crisps and a packet of chicken soup at me. 'It's not what Coach Jenkins would call a good square meal,' he said, 'but it's a start.'

'Gaz,' I said nervously. 'We really should ask Ruthie first.'

'But we can't, can we?' snapped Gareth. 'Because she's just gone and banned us from leaving the kitchen. And anyway, I'm not going near that living room again because there's a bloke in there wearing make-up, riding a unicycle and juggling fireballs. It's a wonder I didn't get my rugby kit scorched. This entire house is a total health and safety hazard.'

Goose was holding up the packet soup against the candle flame and investigating it with interest. She tapped the printed instructions and said, 'It says here we can add an egg to make it thicker, Gaz. Do you reckon you can find one?'

I watched the pair of them helplessly. They were robbing my sister's food and getting on like they were suddenly the best ever friends in the whole of best-ever-friend-land. It was getting on my nerves. I might as well have been at home.

Gareth found a solitary egg in another cupboard and handed it to Goose. 'I don't know how old this egg is,' he said. 'And it hasn't got a date stamped on it. Do you reckon it's worth risking? I don't wanna get the squits.'

And that was when I felt something ping inside my brain. I think it was my patience snapping. I said, 'Hello? Hello? I'm STILL here. I can't believe that all you two can talk about is whether or not to put a stupid egg into some stupid soup! My mum is having an affair with Stevie Wonder! Do you have ANY idea how much that freaks me out? Well, I'll tell you something – You can take your eggs and SPLATTER them for all I care.'

And then Goose did another extraordinary thing. She let go of the egg she'd been holding and sent it crashing to the floor. Even in the candlelight, it looked pretty deliberate to me. Bits of broken egg yolk and slime slithered over the floor tiles.

'What did you do that for?' I said.

And not for the first time that evening, Goose said – or rather shouted, 'I am having an existential crisis!'

And after she'd said this, she started mumbling.

Really fast.

In a manner which was – quite frankly – scary.

And what she mumbled sounded something like this:

'I'm sorry but I just don't know what I'm doing here and I don't even know what the point of my life is any more and I'm trapped in a kitchen inside a house party which I'm not even invited to and I'm getting skin irritations from this hideous polyester uniform and I've probably got the sack from my job for not turning up to work today but the most tragic thing of all is that I don't even care because I hate my job and I only ever see the beginning and end scenes of the films and I spend half my life in the dark and also I'm sick of picking up other people's choc ice wrappers and I work with a woman who has developed her own mumble-language and the worse thing of all is that I'm already totally fluent in it myself . . .'

At this point, she stopped mumbling for a second and looked over at me with big alarmed eyes. 'Oh . . . my . . . God,' she said. 'I spend half my life having muttered conversations in the Ponty-Carlo. Does that mean I'm turning into another Pat Mumble?'

I picked up another cork from the work surface, put it between my teeth and bit it. My mum has always told me that honesty is the best policy. Sometimes, though, I reckon that there are certain occasions when it's better to lie.

'No way,' I said.

'Phew,' said Goose. And then she started mumbling again. 'It gets worse though because even though my job is minging I can't stay away from the place because I'm hopelessly devoted to a boy whose name backwards just happens to be Pure Vomit and it's totally tragically pointless since I've already made a massive mess of everything because yesterday after work I went and told him how I feel and he told me plain and simple that he refuses to consider any serious or frivolous relationship with anyone who isn't yet in sixth form because he is totally turned off by school uniform . . . and I really don't know what to do because I am totally in love with Tim Overup!'

And then she threw back her head and made a big scary noise that was part Ooooooofffffff and part proper scream.

Me and Gareth stared at her in horrified astonishment. In the room next door, somebody was strumming a guitar to the accompaniment of bongo drums and a drunken choir of singing students. But in our kitchen it felt like you could have heard a pin drop. I didn't know what to say. I don't think Gareth did either and he's usually very good in awkward situations. Finally, I took the piece of cork I was biting out from between my teeth and said, 'I wondered if you'd noticed that Tim Overup's name backwards is Pure Vomit. It's unlucky, isn't it?'

Goose said, 'I don't care. I love him. But he doesn't love me.' And then she sank down on to the floor and started crying.

Before I could go and comfort her, Gareth made a groaning noise and said, 'This is the worst party I've ever been to.' Then he walked over to the sink, rinsed out his coffee mug and started to fill it with beer from one of the big plastic bottles on the work surface.

'Gareth David Lloyd George Stingecombe,' I said, 'what the heck do you think you're doing?'

'I'm having a beer,' replied Gareth. 'You two are driving me to drink.'

'But you can't,' I wailed. 'Ruthie will go ballistic.'

Gareth laughed loudly. Too loudly. And then he stopped laughing and said, 'Well, she'll just have to be patient and wait her turn because right now there's a whole queue of people wanting to go ballistic at me.'

'Yeah . . . well . . . alcohol isn't the answer,' I said.

Gareth gave me a long hard look. Then he directed his gaze up to the ceiling and gave Britney Biggs a long hard look too. And after that, he said, 'Oooooooooffffffff,' and tipped his beer down the sink and sank down on the floor next to Goose.

'Goosey?' I said. 'Gazzy?'

'I love him, Lottie,' sobbed Goose. 'Tim Overup is the most individual and unique person that I've ever met. But he's in sixth form and he isn't interested in me.'

'And I'll tell you something else,' said Gareth miserably, 'my rugby career is over.'

Putting both my hands on my head, I said, 'What are you talking about?' I just couldn't keep up with this conversation.

Gareth sniffed and rubbed his nose on the cuff of his rugby shirt. 'It's finished, Lottie! And it never even properly began.'

'Of course it's not over,' I said. 'You told me just the other day that Coach Jenkins reckons you'll get called up to play for the Wales youth team.'

Gareth's head sank into his hands. I looked at him in bewilderment and then, anxiously, I snuck a glance at Goose. She had her arms wrapped around her shins and was all hunched forward so that *her* face was pressed against the tops of her knees. I think that – ever so slightly – she may have been rocking backwards and forwards. Generally, this isn't a good sign. She certainly didn't look happy. Neither did Gareth. Which leads me to conclude that he was bang-on accurate with his earlier assessment: This really was THE WORST PARTY EVER.

'The thing is . . .' said Gareth in an oddly strangled voice, 'I did get that call-up, Lottie.'

'Well, that's brilliant,' I said. 'So why the face like a half-chewed chip?'

'Because,' said Gareth, still in that weird husky voice, '. . . because . . . instead of turning up for my first training session at the Millennium Stadium, I bumped into you and ended up at this poxy party!'

I stared at him in horror. My stomach hurt. Just like someone had kicked me. In a voice that sounded even more oddly strangled than Gareth's, I said, 'Why didn't you tell me?'

'I tried to,' said Gareth.

I couldn't think of anything good to say so I said, 'Whoops!'

'Yeah,' said Gareth. 'Whoops. They're never going to want me now. Coach Jenkins reckons you don't get anywhere in this world if you're not reliable.'

'I didn't make you come with me, Gaz,' I said and nervously jiggled the corks in my pocket. I wasn't deliberately shouting at him but my voice – all by itself – had gone up a few octaves. 'In actual fact, I didn't even ask you.'

'Yeah, I know,' said Gareth and breathed out a great big noisy sigh. 'But it's not as simple as that, is it? I was so completely panicked about the idea of you and Goose clearing off out of Cardiff without telling anyone that I had to do something! You weren't even wearing a coat.' And then he looked me right in the eye. Gareth has got very beautiful green eyes. Even in the dim candlelight, I could see that. Without really knowing why, I held my breath. Gareth bit his lip and then took a deep breath and said,

'You're my girlfriend, Lottie – and I love you.'

'Oh my God,' whispered Goose through her sobs. 'That is the sweetest thing I have EVER heard.'

'I've been trying to say that for ages,' said Gareth, wiping his face on the sleeve of his rugby shirt. 'But it kept coming out wrong.' He puffed out his cheeks in what I can only describe as an expression of pure and total frustration. 'I always thought it would be a totally amazing moment when I first ever said those words to anyone – but actually, it's just rubbish.' Then he gave a big sniff, put his hands over his eyes and left them there.

And I'm pretty sure that it was at this point that I started to cry too because suddenly everything had got way too intense and very very confusing.

And even though all I can do is live my life in forward gear, it makes a helluva lot more sense when I think about it now in reverse. Food deprivation and oxygen starvation had nothing to do with why Goose, Gareth and I went so utterly mad on Sunday night. And I can't even blame Michel. As much as I hate to admit it, I think that my wiser and cleverer sister Ruthie had correctly understood the situation right from the start.

It was my fault.

I'd run away from home and – without any thought for either of them – I'd dragged Goose and Gareth along to support me.

And the eight cups of coffee probably didn't help much either.

there are BIG shIPs aND smaLL shIPs . . .

It's just gone three o'clock and I've been joined in the library by two girls who have creatively teamed treggings and knuggs[26] with their school uniforms. They are huddled together in front of a single computer and every two seconds they collapse with attacks of laughter. To be honest, this is fairly annoying because we're in a library and anyone with half a head knows that libraries are supposed to be areas of quiet study. It's making it very difficult for me to concentrate and this is having a detrimental impact on the flow of my stream of consciousness. I *was* going to write about how Goose and Gareth and I woke up on Monday morning with frayed nerves and humongous coffee headaches and about how my dad drove all the way down to Aberystwyth from Wrexham to pick me up and take me back to North Wales with him. Oh, and I was also going to write about Ruthie and how she ended up going home for Christmas earlier than she'd ever planned because she insisted on accompanying Goose and Gareth back to Cardiff so that they wouldn't miss another day of double science with Mr Thomas. I was going to write about these things but now I'm not because the two giggling girls opposite are putting me right off.

---

[26] Are you searching for that casual comfort of leggings combined with the smart styling of a trouser? Then you need treggings! I'm not going to explain the knuggs thing all over again.

So instead I'll write about them.

Thankfully, they have stopped shrieking with laughter and one of the girls – who has blatantly cut her own fringe – is telling the other girl – who is wearing a candy necklace that she is in the process of eating – about someone called Pot-Wash-Pete. Their conversation is running pretty much along the lines of this:

DIY Fringe:	Yeah, so I was in the middle of my waitressing shift and Pot-Wash-Pete said, 'Do you wanna come to the cinema with me on Saturday? There's this really freaky film showing called *And They Died Screaming*. It's supposed to be the scariest thing ever.'
Candy Necklace:	Oh my God!!! You're not seriously contemplating a date with Pot-Wash-Pete, are you? That boy is an environmental hazard. He's polluting the world with a serious geek leak!
DIY Fringe:	Ahhh ha ha ha behave. He's a really sweet person!
Candy Necklace:	Oh my God!!! You do, don't you? You fancy Pot-Wash-Pete?
DIY Fringe:	Get real. This is Pot-Wash-Pete we're talking about.
Candy Necklace:	So what did you say to him?
DIY Fringe:	I told him to trot off. Look, it's nearly

	three fifteen. Let's go into town. The shops are gonna be shutting soon and I need to buy something.
Candy Necklace:	Like what?
DIY Fringe:	I dunno. Just anything.

And now they've both got up and rushed straight out of the library. And the weird thing is, that despite the fact that they were getting on my nerves, I'm actually rather sorry to see them go. Even though their conversation was frankly quite pointless, they seemed like OK people. I should've warned them how bad that film is. And also, I think I'd have quite liked to rush into town with them. Because I like buying anything as well.

But the truth is that I don't have anyone to rush into town with.

It's got me thinking again about that tea towel on the wall of The Good Friends Cafe. There was a lot of truth written on that tea towel. There *are* big ships and there *are* small ships but, in the great big scheme of things, they don't matter all that much. Without big ships we wouldn't have any Caribbean cruises. Without small ships, we wouldn't have any cruises around Cardiff Bay. Big deal.

The most important ship of all is friendship. And friendship floats my boat.

It's cheesier than Cheddar but it's true.

I haven't got any friends here and it's a very lonely state of affairs. It's giving me that spaceman feeling again.

And even worse than that, it's making me feel a lot like that solitary swinging girl in that weird film I watched the other day.

And what's even worse than that is that every time I swing forward, I'm confronted with this terrible truth in massive letters, which is staring me straight in the face:

I haven't been showing that much consideration to Gareth or Goose.

And every time I swing backwards, I get a glimpse of an even more terrible truth – but this time it's in hazy distant faraway letters because it's something I've shoved to the back of my head in the hope that it might go away.

But it won't go away. It's this:

I haven't been showing that much consideration to my mum either.

And this whole minging swinging sensation in my head might be discombobulating but it has made me realize something important. It's made me realize that rather than sitting here feeling sorry for myself, it's high time that I went home and sorted one or two things out.

CONtemPLatING MY CONuNDrums aND DeaLING wIth MY DILemmas

It already seems like a billion zillion years ago but it was only the other day that I was worrying my head off over a series of conundrums which were causing me an uncomfortable amount of concern. I think I finally have a few of the answers.

1. **What do I *really* want to be given for Christmas this year?**

Actually, I don't mind. I'd be happy with more or less anything. A nine-inch flat-screen television would be fantastic of course, and so would a laptop – but, to be honest, they are just luxurious trimmings. I probably don't *really* need them. Not like I need my hair-straighteners and a coat that doesn't smell of mud and my own room where I can keep all my stuff and a house where I'm welcome at any time of the day – even between the hours of 9 a.m. and 4 p.m. – and where there's absolutely no danger of my presence damaging anyone's online herbal remedy business. *These* are the sorts of things that are essential to the smooth running of my life. I'd still really like an orang-utan adoption pack though. And some false eyelashes.

2. What am I going to give other people?

The only person I've asked so far is my mum. She said she'd like the latest CD by Susan Boyle. Personally, I'd be happier buying her Lady Gaga or Kings of Leon but if it's Boyley she wants, it's Boyley she'll have. Gareth is going to get the rugby-themed T-shirt I bought for him in Wrexham. What I'm going to give everybody else remains a mystery.

3. How am I going to give them anything at all when I don't actually have any money?

This is also a problematic mystery. I'm quite a creative person though so I'm sure I'll think of something. In fact, my art teacher, Mr Spanton, has said every single year in my school report that I have *a naturally artistic streak*. So maybe the solution is to make a few things. I reckon I could make my brother Caradoc a really good Darth Vader mask and I think I'd quite like to make my sister Ruthie a cork noticeboard for her to attach all her library fines to. I saw one being made on the telly once out of wine-bottle corks. What you do is cut all the corks in half and glue them to a flat piece of wood. I know it sounds rubbish but it actually looks incredibly stylish. When I was in the kitchen at Ruthie's student house the other day, I collected sixty-eight wine-bottle corks so I should have more than enough to complete the job. Unfortunately, the Susan Boyle CD will have to come out of my pocket money.

4. As a follower of the philosophy of René Descartes, should I even bother to celebrate Christmas anyway? After all, the only thing that I can be truly certain of is my own existence.

The short answer is yes. The longer answer is that, whilst I have the utmost respect for Monsieur Descartes and his philosophical theories, I have discovered a basic and fundamental flaw in his logic. And it's this:

If I go through life believing that *I* am the only thing which actually exists, I am in serious danger of deteriorating into a one-way talker.

This would be very bad.

One-way talkers are those annoying people who strut about this planet talking at everyone and believing that they are tastier than a bar of chocolate. As well as being colossally boring, these people are also in serious danger of bumping into a lamp post or getting themselves run over because they're so busy marvelling at the magnificence of their own belly buttons that they don't pay any attention to where they're going.

The awful thing is, that just recently I think I've been guilty of this myself. I've been so wrapped up in my own existence that, for a while, I stopped considering the existence of everyone else.

Yes, it's true that . . .

I write therefore I am!

. . . but it's equally true that Gareth David Lloyd George Stingecombe plays rugby – therefore *he is*. And if I'd bothered to ask him why he was wearing his training kit on the bus to the city centre last Sunday lunchtime, he'd probably be playing for the Wales youth team by now. And then there's Goose. She's my best friend and I never even spotted that she was having an existential crisis of a reasonably significant nature triggered by the fact that she is hideously and hopelessly and head-over-heels in love with Tim Overup – the sixth-form film fanatic who refuses to consider any serious or frivolous relationship with anyone still legally obliged to wear a school uniform. I should have done.

And finally, there's my mum. For fifteen and a half years, I've honestly believed that her philosophy on life went pretty much like this:

I am Lottie's mum therefore I am.

Or at a push, perhaps:

I catch criminals therefore I am!

But in all the time that I've been alive, it's never occurred to me until now that my mum is actually a much more complicated individual who has her own conundrums and dilemmas to deal with. Just like I have. If my RE teacher, Mr Davies, was here, he'd probably put two fingers on his pursed lips and then, after a big thoughtful pause, say something along the lines of, 'Your . . . mum . . . is . . . unique. *Hmmm? Hmmm?* Consider that, Lottie. *Hmmm?* There's nobody else quite like her on the entire planet.' And he'd be bang on target, of course. She *is* unique. And complicated. And I realize now that she is a normal woman in the grip of a womanly urge. And to be honest, if Stevie Wonder can help her tackle this urge then who am I to kick up a fuss?

And, all in all, what I'm trying to say is that whilst I'm still very interested in the things that René Descartes has to say, I wouldn't exactly describe myself as a *follower* of his philosophy any more. Because I think that it may possibly have been a load of old twonk and certainly not worth cancelling Christmas for. Besides, when I was in Wrexham library yesterday, I read that René was actually an extremely religious man, so – regardless of whatever he told all of us – *he* must have believed he wasn't the only thing on this planet. And I bet he didn't cancel his Christmas either.

But the dilemma that was doing my head in the most was this one:

5. Who will I be spending Christmas Day with this year?

And now I've got it all sorted out in my mind. Because, at the end of the day, when all is said and done, I now know, without any shadow of doubt, that I will be spending it . . .

Here

Where I belong.

And where I am right now.

In my house. 62 Springfield Place, Whitchurch, Cardiff, Wales, United Kingdom, Europe, Planet Earth, The Universe. With my mum and Ruthie and Winnie the elderly chinchilla.

And yes . . . on Christmas Day, I'll be with Steve and Lois as well.

But I'm actually feeling fairly relaxed about this because yesterday, on the train back from Wrexham, I did some serious and intense thinking. To be honest, there was nothing else to do. The journey from Wrexham General to Cardiff Central takes three hours and I didn't have my MP3 player with me. In fact, I didn't have very much with me at all. My dad had lent me a holdall but the only things I'd put inside it were Gareth's rugby training top, the T-shirts I'd bought from the Butchers' Market and a load of corks that I'd collected from Ruthie's party. I think it's fair to say that just recently I've been travelling very light.

My dad dropped me off at the train station on his way to work. Before I got out of his car, he said, 'Are you sure you don't want to stay here? At least until Saturday? I could drive you back to Cardiff then. It would save you having to sit on the train all by yourself.'

'Thanks,' I said. 'But I really need to go *now*. I've already missed four days of school. Tomorrow is the last day before we break up for the holidays and I want to be there. And in the evening, there's going to be an end-of-term disco and everything.'

My dad said, 'You really should have thought about all of that before you went charging off to Aberystwyth, shouldn't you?'

'Yes,' I said. Because he was right.

My dad looked sad and picked at a loose bit of thread on his steering wheel. 'I'm sorry you got left on your own a bit this week. But I can't just take days off work willy-nilly whenever I want to.'

'It's all right, Dad,' I said.

'And Sally *is* very busy with her online herbal remedies business, but perhaps she should have spent a little extra time with you.'

I pulled a face.

My dad said, 'What are you pulling a face for?'

My mum has always told me that honesty is the best policy but I reckon that this was another one of those occasions when it's better to lie.

'My cheek was feeling a bit stiff,' I said.

'Oh,' said my dad, and nodded. Then, after a pause, he said, 'Be good then. And phone me when you get back.'

'I will,' I said. And then I gave him a big hug before taking my half-empty holdall out of the back of the car and walking away to find my train.

That was about eight o'clock this morning. It's just gone 8 p.m. now and I definitely feel an entire twelve hours older than I did back then.

To begin with, I think it was the worry that aged me. As the train pulled out of Wrexham, all I could think about was my mum who'd be waiting for me at the other end of the line. I hadn't seen her since that hideous row we'd had at the breakfast table. That was four days ago. I'd spoken to her on the phone a couple of times but, even from a distance of approximately one hundred and seven miles, I could tell that my mum wasn't particularly chuffed with me. As I sat all on my lonesome on that train which was bringing me closer and closer to the face-on fury of my mum, I started to get uncomfortably tense. For a while, I gazed out of the window and tried not to think about it. There was some very nice scenery to look at. The hills outside Wrexham are much bigger than the hills outside Cardiff. And they're darker and sharper and much more dramatic looking. I suppose they might technically even be mountains. I stared at these mini-mountains for ages and actually, to begin with, I found it quite a calming experience. But then it started raining and the sky went all murky and grey and the window I was looking out of became so splattered with big fat raindrops that I couldn't actually see clearly. And then, for some weird reason, I swear to God, I started to spot my mum's face everywhere. Sometimes she was peering back at me from the reflection in the glass of the train's window, and other times she was hiding in the clouds and peeping over the tops of the mountains. Sort of like this:

And this wasn't very relaxing at all so I stopped looking out of the window and closed my eyes and attempted to go to sleep instead. But that didn't work either because instead of seeing the usual dark nothing that you expect to find when you close your eyes, I saw weird floating images like this:

So then I tried crossing my eyes and holding my breath but that was actually the most useless idea of all because the only effect it had was to make me go completely dizzy and start coughing and, rather than making me forget about my mum, the inside of my head filled up with this:

But thankfully, just as I was on the verge of real panic, we pulled into the big busy station at Shrewsbury, and so many people got on and off the train that I was totally distracted and all those terrifying mini-mums in my mind went running off to chase a few mini-criminals. Opposite me, a couple of shemos sat down. They were both about Ruthie's age and they were wearing black eye make-up and black lipstick and had lots of piercings stuck into their faces. I was slightly scared of them so I zipped myself up inside the snorkel hood of my sister's muddy parka and made them disappear from view. I could still hear them though. In a surprisingly cheerful voice, one of them said, 'I can't wait for tomorrow night. My mum is having a *Mamma Mia!* party. I reckon it's going to be a hoot.'

Inside the muddy parka, I stiffened. For some reason, this opening line of conversation caught me totally by surprise. I think I'd been expecting them to talk about death.

The other shemo said, 'Excellent! I love all those Abba songs. When it came out, I took my gran to the big multi-screen cinema to see it. She said it was the first time she'd been to the pictures for more than thirty years. She loved it! We were both singing along with all the songs and everything. I'm going to visit her on Sunday and I'm taking the DVD of *Free Willy* with me. I reckon she'd really like that film as well.'

'Bound to,' said the first shemo. 'It's a killer whale-based aquatic classic.' And then, through the long tunnel of my snorkel hood, I sneakily watched as she took a big packet of marshmallows out of her bag and began sharing them with her friend.

Inside my parka, I still hadn't moved a muscle. I think I was in a state of shock. Apart from those two hopeless conversational exchanges I'd had with Lois, this was the first time I'd ever heard emos communicating. And, to be honest, I'd never expected them to sound so . . . well . . . normal.

And then I immediately felt cross with myself because you don't have to be a brainiac or a rocket scientist to know that there's no such blinking thing as normal anyway.

Feeling stupid, I unzipped my snorkel hood and re-entered the world. The shemo who owned the marshmallows looked over at me and smiled. 'I wondered if there was anyone inside that big coat,' she said. Then she held out her packet of marshmallows to me and added, 'Want one?'

'Ta,' I said and took one.

After that, she went back to discussing *Mamma Mia!* and *Free Willy* with her friend and I went right on back to staring out of the window. But this time, instead of constantly seeing my mum everywhere, the only person's face I could see peeping back at me was Lois's.

And I started to wonder about whether I'd ever really given her a fair chance. My initial reaction was this:

OMG, totally! She's been a complete crabby knickers every single time I've spoken to her.

But then I started thinking about how she was only the same age as me and she'd already lost her mum. And even though I had a big fat marshmallow slowly melting in my mouth, this made me feel hideously sad and awful because if *I* was Lois *I'd* probably feel pretty cheesed off with the whole world and dress in nothing but black clothes all the time too. I once read somewhere that after Prince Albert died, Queen Victoria dressed like a shemo for forty entire years!

Fact!

And making that tiny extra effort to get inside the heads of Lois Giles and Queen Victoria definitely had some kind of hardcore emotional effect on me because I suddenly felt a whole lot older and wiser. Right then and there on that train, I realized that my mum was absolutely right to insist that Lois should join us on Christmas Day. After all, she could hardly stay at home like the Lone Ranger, could she? And that just got me thinking about what a nice, caring and considerate person my mum actually is and how much I couldn't wait to see her again. And when my train finally pulled into Cardiff Central station, my mum was waiting on the platform to meet me and I gave her the biggest tightest bear hug that you could possibly give a person without doing them some serious spinal damage.

aPOLOGIes . . .

I am who I am . . .

And who I am is someone who is wrong occasionally.

Without any shadow of a doubt, this has been one of those occasions. Yesterday, after we'd got back from the train station, I made a big blotchy-faced apology to my mum. She listened quietly to what I had to say and then she said, 'We all make mistakes, Lottie. The important thing is not to go on making those same thoughtless mistakes over and over again.' And then she gave me her police sergeant look and said, 'But understand this – if you run off like that again, I'm going to sell you on eBay. And I seriously mean that.'

My sister, Ruthie, who was sitting in the next room and blatantly earwigging our private conversation, chipped in at that point and shouted through the open doorway, 'She's not worth the trouble, Mum. You wouldn't get any bids.'

'Keep your beak out, Big Bird,' I shouted back.

'Oh wind your neck in, Beryl,' said Ruthie.

This made me go quiet. Beryl is my official middle name but it upsets me to be reminded of this fact.

My mum looked up at the ceiling and said, 'Oh for goodness sake! Is it unreasonable to expect you two to like each other?'

Ruthie appeared in the doorway with a look of horror on her face. 'Get real – I don't like her,' she said. 'She's my squid sister.' And then Ruthie winked at me and said, 'But I love her to bits. Obviously.'

'Fish-breath,' I muttered under my breath. I was smiling though. I couldn't help it.

'Squid,' said Ruthie.

'Get out of my kitchen, the pair of you,' said my mum. And as I went hurrying off up the stairs to my room, I heard her say to Ruthie, 'You're twenty years old. When are you going to start acting as if you are?'

And this made me chuckle because I can't ever imagine Ruthie being all grown-up and boring, which is probably why I love her to bits.

In contrast, my friend Goose is only fifteen but she's got her foot to the floor in the fastest car on the motorway to middle-age . . . and I love *her* to bits too. When we were walking to school together this morning, I asked her how things were at the Ponty-Carlo Picture House.

'Pat Mumble fired me,' she said.

'Whoops,' I said. 'That was probably my fault, wasn't it?'

'Don't worry,' shrugged Goose. 'I would've left anyway. The lack of daylight was turning me into a vampire and giving me a Vitamin D deficiency . . . and anyway, the situation between me and Tim Overup was totally untenable.'

Goose is very good with words. At the time, I didn't know what *untenable* meant so I just nodded sympathetically. But a little while ago, I looked it up in a dictionary and it said this:

unte´nable *adjective* being without a base; incapable of being maintained or defended; groundless; unsound

. . . which doesn't leave me a whole lot wiser.

'To be honest, Goose,' I said, 'I didn't think he really seemed your type.'

Goose shrugged again. 'That's *why* I like him. He's totally different to anyone I've ever been out with. He's mature and thoughtful, he knows loads about books and films and art, and he totally does his own thing and doesn't fit into any poxy pointless pigeonholes.'

I thought about this for a while and, while I was thinking, we walked along in silence. Finally, I said, 'So does that make him a Type A, Type B or Type C person?'

Goose laughed. 'I don't know. But who honestly cares?'

And even though I was a bit confused, I smiled back and said, 'No one, I suppose.'

We walked along in silence for a bit more and then I said, 'So what are you going to do about it?'

'Nothing,' said Goose. 'I'm just gonna live each day as it comes and then when I'm a bit older and a bit more grown-up, I'll see if he's changed his mind.'

'Yeah,' I said, '. . . but you might have changed your mind about him by then. Or fallen in love with somebody else. Or moved to Kentucky. Or anything. Life can only be understood backwards but it has to be lived forwards, you know.'

Goose stopped walking and looked at me, a hint of a grin on her face. 'True. You're very wise sometimes, Lottie Biggs. Do you know that?'

'Am I?' I said, genuinely confused. 'I don't think so! If I was wise I wouldn't have run off to Aberystwyth without telling my mum and I wouldn't have dragged you along with me as back-up and, if I really *was* wise, I'd certainly have noticed that you were having an existential crisis in the middle of my sister's grotty kitchen.' And then I said, 'I'm truly sorry. I honestly am.'

Goose put her head on one side and smiled. Just for a moment, she reminded me of my mum. But then she stuck her tongue out and went boss-eyed and any similarity to my mum instantly vanished. 'It's OK,' she said. 'Just don't do it again.'

'I won't,' I said, and I meant it. 'Honestly, Goose, friends like you can't just be ordered out of a catalogue, can they?'

This time it was Goose's turn to look confused. But only for a second. Then a sparkle appeared in each of her eyes and, linking her arm through mine, we continued on our way in the direction of school.

We hadn't gone more than a few paces though before the ting-a-ling of a bicycle bell stopped us in our tracks and caused us to spin round. Behind us, weaving dangerously on an ancient black bike, was Tim Overup. Flashing us both an awkward grin, he scraped his shoe along the pavement until he wobbled to an awkward halt. Then he leaned forward awkwardly on to his handlebars, pushed a stray piece of awkward gingery hair away from his eyes, and awkwardly asked, 'Gail, might I have a quick word?'

I snuck a glance at Goose. Goose hates being called by

her proper name. It can make her turn quite chopsy. To be fair, she didn't look like she was turning chopsy just then but she had gone very still and very red and her mouth was hanging slightly open. I nudged her and her mouth snapped shut.

Tim Overup fiddled with his fringe again, gave another nervous smile and said, 'Er . . . Gail . . . I won't keep you long. It's just that . . . um . . . well . . . I've been thinking about our last conversation and I can't help thinking that I've been a bit of an idiot . . . I'm really sorry and . . . well . . . I was wondering if there was any chance . . . any chance at all that you'd . . .'

'Yes,' said Goose, suddenly finding her voice again.

Tim Overup blinked. And then he smiled. And this time, it wasn't a small nervous smile – it was a great big happy and relieved one. It actually made him look rather nice.

'Fantastic,' said Tim. 'I've got your phone number. I'll call you later, shall I?'

'Yes,' said Goose, who now had a great big happy smile on her face too.

'Fantastic,' said Tim, again. 'That's really fantastic.' And then he put his hand into the pocket of his jumbo cords and pulled out a crumpled page of newspaper. 'I . . . er . . . don't know if you're interested but . . .'

'I am,' interrupted Goose.

Tim did a funny little laugh. And this time, it sounded less like the funny harrumphing giraffe-laugh that I'd heard him do on the bus that other time and much more like a very sweet happy hiccup. He handed her the page from the newspaper and said, 'There's a film on at Movie World called *Love, Lies and Secrets*. This review in *The Western Mail* described it as the romance of the year. We could go and see it together if you like?'

Goose smiled so widely that it looked like her face was splitting in half. 'I would DEFINITELY like,' she said.

'Fantastic,' said Tim for the billionth time. 'I'll call you later then, Gail.' And then he made that sweet little happy hiccup noise, climbed back on to his ancient saddle and pedalled off towards the sixth-form centre. For a moment, Goose stood rooted to the spot with a weird faraway look on her face and watched him disappear down the road. Then she said, 'Am I dreaming?'

'Nope,' I said.

'Fantastic,' said Goose. 'Fan–flipping–tastic.' And with that weird faraway look still firmly plastered all over her face, she said, 'He calls me Gail. How utterly romantic is that?'

'Is it?' I said. 'I thought you hated being called Gail.'

'Not by him I don't,' said Goose, and then she threaded her arm back through mine and we finished the final half-mile to school propelled through the air on a whirlwind of love and optimism.

. . . aND haPPY eNDINGs

When we reached the upper school teaching block, I said bye to Goose and we went our separate ways. She headed off to her form room and I headed off to the tuck shop where I guessed I'd find Gareth somewhere close to the front of the queue. Sure enough, he was being served just as I arrived. I stood to one side of the queue and waited as he took his change and a steaming hot dog from Mr Doughnut. Inside my pockets, the fingers on both my hands were crossed. I'm not sure why. I don't think that crossing your fingers actually achieves anything.

Gareth turned away from the serving hatch and raised his hot dog to his mouth. And then, seeing me, he stopped. My fingers crossed even tighter and my mouth went a bit dry.

Gareth nodded. 'All right, Biggsy?'

'All right, Gaz?' I said.

Gareth nodded again. 'So you came back then?'

'Hmm,' I said.

'Good,' said Gareth. 'I'm glad about that.' And then he gave me a small awkward smile and turned away and began to walk towards our form room.

I panicked. 'Gareth,' I shouted. 'Don't go!' Several people who were waiting in the queue for the tuck shop looked over at us. Gareth paused and turned back to look at me. His face had gone very red. I think mine had too because I suddenly felt abnormally sweaty.

'Gareth,' I said, quieter. 'I want to say sorry.'

Gareth kicked at the ground with his foot. 'It's OK. Doesn't matter now.'

'No,' I said. 'It's not OK and it does matter. If I hadn't been such a one-way talker, you'd be playing for the Wales youth team by now.'

Gareth looked at his uneaten hot dog. 'Coach Jenkins says I might get another chance.'

'I've bought you something,' I said. 'It was meant to be a Christmas present really but I think you should have it now.' I unzipped my coat and pulled out a stripy red carrier bag that I'd been carrying under my jumper.

Gareth looked at the bag and bit his lip. 'Oh, I dunno—'

'Please, Gaz,' I said. 'Take it.'

Gareth hesitated. Then he put his hot dog into my hand, took the bag from me and pulled out the T-shirt that was inside it.

A small hint of a smile played on his lips.

'The thing is, Gaz . . .' I said, suddenly speaking really quickly and really nervously, '. . . the thing is . . . if we're going to carry on going out with each other, I think there have to be certain rules . . . and the first rule is that you've got to take your rugby career seriously and not go running off to Aberystwyth with me at the drop of a hat. You've got to be focused . . . You mustn't let women . . . and that includes me . . . get in the way of your passion for the game. Because rugby is not a pastime, Gareth, it's a way of life.'

Gareth nodded slowly. The hint of a smile was still on his lips. 'OK, Coach,' he said.

Still clutching Gareth's hot dog, I took a deep breath. I wasn't finished yet. 'And also,' I said, 'I was wondering if you're still going to the end-of-term disco tonight . . . because if you are . . . and if you don't mind . . . I'd really like to go with you.'

Gareth frowned. I felt my heart sink. He began kicking at the ground again and said, 'Oh I dunno, Lottie. To be honest, I'm thinking I might go night-fishing with my mate, Spud, instead. I've been spending too much time around girls recently. It's given me a seriously bad attack of the Frillies.'

'Oh,' I said. 'OK then.' I could hardly speak. My jaw had locked and my heart had stopped. I guess that this is what it feels like to be dumped by someone you really really like.

Gareth scratched his chin as if he was turning over something in his mind. Finally, he said, 'But seeing as it's you who's asking, I think I'll give the night-fishing a miss.'

I stared at him. 'You're not dumping me?'

Gareth said, 'Don't be daft!' And then he took his hot dog out of my hands and ate it.

I did a funny little laugh. I couldn't stop myself. It was like a sudden unstoppable happy hiccup. We began walking together towards our form room. I took a deep breath. I still wasn't finished yet. 'Gaz,' I said, 'can I ask you something?'

Gareth looked at me warily. 'Depends what it is.'

'Well,' I said, '. . . you know when we were in Ruthie's kitchen the other day . . .'

'Ain't likely to forget,' interrupted Gareth. 'Worst party ever!'

'Well,' I said, '. . . you were explaining about why you came with me to Aberystwyth and you used this small word beginning with L . . .'

Gareth butted in. 'Leeks?'

'No, not leeks . . .'

'Lunch?'

'No, you said . . .'

Gareth continued to interrupt me. 'Lollipop? Lard? Lobster?'

I stopped walking. Gareth stopped too. Standing on tiptoes so that I could reach his ear with my mouth, I whispered, 'You said you loved me. Is that true?'

Gareth's ear turned bright pink and so did the rest of his face.

I took another deep breath and put my hand up to his cheek so that I could turn his face towards mine. Our eyes met. Gareth has got very beautiful green eyes and even though those eyes are more than capable of completely fuddling my brain, there was no way that I was going to get fuddled right then.

'I love you, Gareth Stingecombe,' I said.

Gareth's green eyes widened. For a moment, he seemed to freeze in shock. And then, to my enormous relief, the hint of a smile that had been playing on his lips for some time grew into a great big lovely one. Cupping my face in his hands, he said, '*This* has got to be the most amazing moment ever!' And then, right in the middle of the schoolyard, he kissed me and we stood there swapping the most intense and incredible kisses until Mrs Rowlands, the Welsh teacher, told us to stop being inappropriate and get to registration.

And even though that was, without doubt, the best thing that happened to me today, it wasn't the only highlight. Before I finish writing, there is something else I need to mention. On our way home from school, Goose and I spotted Elvis Presley standing on the traffic island in the middle of Whitchurch village. He was singing a song through his traffic cone to the people who were passing by. I turned to Goose and said, 'I know this seems a bit random but I just need to have a quick word with Elvis.'

Goose looked gobsmacked. 'I wouldn't have thought he was your type,' she said.

I grinned. 'Oh, jog on, Goose. You know I'm not interested in types.'

We came to a stop by his bench. Through his vibrating traffic cone, Elvis said, 'Hello there, little lady, are you feeling a bit more cheerful today?'

'Yeah,' I said. 'But can you put your traffic cone down for a second, please, Elvis, because otherwise everyone in Whitchurch Village can hear.'

'Fair enough,' said Elvis and put his traffic cone beside him on the bench. 'Is it a special request you're after?'

'No,' I said. 'I just wanted to say thank you for talking to me the other day when I was really depressed, and for telling me about Socrates and life's rich tapestry and examining the knots and everything. I didn't fully appreciate it at the time but I did later on . . . when I'd had a chance to properly think about it all.'

Elvis waved my thanks away with his hand. 'My pleasure,' he said.

'Oh, and I got you a Christmas present,' I said.

Elvis looked surprised. So did Goose. I unzipped my coat and pulled out a second T-shirt that I'd been carrying around with me all day. This one had been stuffed between my arm and the sleeve of my coat. You have to be quite creative when you don't carry a school bag.

I passed the T-shirt to Elvis. He took it from me and looked at it. It was the T-shirt I'd had custom-made in Wrexham.

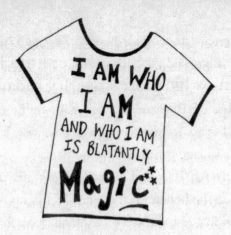

I AM WHO I AM AND WHO I AM IS BLATANTLY Magic

To be honest, I'd had half a mind to give it to Goose. She's definitely magic so she certainly deserves to wear it. But somehow, I felt that Elvis might benefit from it more. And anyway, it was way too big for Goose.

Elvis Presley looked at the T-shirt, astonishment on his face. After a moment or two, he said, 'This is for me?'

'Yeah,' I said. 'I think it will suit you better than that T-shirt that says *I drink therefore I am.*'

Elvis reddened and looked down at a couple of empty beer cans that were resting by his feet. 'Oh, I dunno. It's very nice of you. But I don't think this *magic* stuff really applies to me, does it?'

I shrugged. 'Why not?' I said. 'I'm not much of a philosopher but I truly believe that the only person who can ultimately determine *who* or *what* we are is ourselves.'

Elvis looked even more astonished. 'Crikey,' he said finally. 'I didn't think they taught you kids anything at school any more.' He smiled and then, to my utter delight, he pulled the T-shirt over his head and put it on over the top of his leather jacket. 'Perhaps you're right,' he said. 'And even if you're not, thank you very much!' Then with a big smile, he picked up his traffic cone and began singing some random happy song at the top of his voice.

Goose and I continued on our way home and I had tea with my mum and Ruthie – and in about two hours' time Gareth Stingecombe is going to knock on my door and take me with him to the end-of-term disco where he'll probably do bad beatboxing with Spud to all the Christmas hits on the CD player but still manage to make me the proudest and happiest girl in the entire school.

And there's not much more to say really . . . except for one more very important apology.

And this time it's to an elderly chinchilla who is currently sitting on my lap as I type all this into my computer. Because anyone with half a head knows that every pet deserves an owner who is totally devoted to them. So . . .

I'm sorry, Winnie, for running away and neglecting you and I PROMISE that it won't EVER happen again.

And Winnie, who is probably the Wisest Chinchilla in the Whole of Wales, has just made a sweet chirping noise and bounced on to my desk to lick my hand. So I think this means I'm forgiven. And I'm really glad about that because Winnie's opinion matters to me. He's part of my world. And so is Ruthie and my mum and Goose and Gareth and even Elvis and Stevie and Lois. And to be honest, I think my life would be totally tragic and ridonkulous and untenable without them.

Hayley Long

would like to give a BIG HUG
to the following lush individuals:

Hayley Yeeles at Pollinger;

Emma Young, Rachel Petty and all the hip
young groovers at Macmillan;

Gwen Davies for genius back-up and
advice on the Welsh language;

Scott and Mel Thomas for
science advice;

Helen Floyd for spiritual advice;

Kirsty Price for being . . .
absolutely . . . unique . . . hmmmm?

Erzsébet Horváth for help with the
Hungarian language;

Inkymole for introducing me to the joys of jeggings;

Sophie Kenyon, who won a competition
on MyKindaBook.com and invented the
film *Love, lies and secrets*;

Paston College, Norfolk,
for allowing me to write *and* teach;

my mum, who knows what I'm like;

my bloke, GRAHAM, for being
absolutely amazing . . .

. . . and last, but *not* least, all of YOU who keep sending me
such sweet and lovely messages.

Thank you so much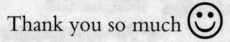

www.hayleylong.com